**Samuel Langhorne Clemens** (November 30, 1835 – April 21, 1910), known by his pen name Mark Twain, was an American writer, humorist, entrepreneur, publisher, and lecturer. He was lauded as the "greatest humorist this country has produced", and William Faulkner called him "the father of American literature". His novels include The Adventures of Tom Sawyer (1876) and its sequel, the Adventures of Huckleberry Finn (1884), the latter often called "The Great American Novel".

Twain was raised in Hannibal, Missouri, which later provided the setting for Tom Sawyer and Huckleberry Finn. He served an apprenticeship with a printer and then worked as a typesetter, contributing articles to the newspaper of his older brother Orion Clemens. He later became a riverboat pilot on the Mississippi River before heading west to join Orion in Nevada. (Source: Wikipedia)

**Literary works:**
The Gilded Age: A Tale of Today (1873)
The Prince and the Pauper (1881)
A Connecticut Yankee in
King Arthur's Court (1889)
The American Claimant (1892)
Pudd'nhead Wilson (1894)
Personal Recollections of Joan of Arc (1896)
A Horse's Tale (1907)
The Mysterious Stranger (1916, posthumous)
The Adventures of Tom Sawyer (1876)
Adventures of Huckleberry Finn (1884)
Tom Sawyer Abroad (1894)
Tom Sawyer, Detective (1896)
"Eve's Diary" (1906)

# In Defense of Harriet Shelley
MARK TWAIN

PRINCE CLASSICS

### PRINCE CLASSICS

This is a work of fiction. Names, characters, places, and incidents either are the product of the author's imagination or are used fictitiously. Any resemblance to actual persons, living or dead, events, or locales is entirely coincidental.

Copyright © 2020

All rights reserved. No part of this book may be reproduced in any form or by any electronic or mechanical means including information storage and retrieval systems, without permission in writing from the author. The only exception is by a reviewer, who may quote short excerpts in a review.

First Printing: 2020

ISBN 978-93-89682-74-8 (paperback)

ISBN 978-93-89682-75-5 (Hardcover)

Published by Prince Classics

www.princeclassics.com

# Contents

I ......................................................................... 9

II ........................................................................ 22

III ....................................................................... 36

About Author ..................................................... 57

# In Defense of
# Harriet Shelley

# I

I have committed sins, of course; but I have not committed enough of them to entitle me to the punishment of reduction to the bread and water of ordinary literature during six years when I might have been living on the fat diet spread for the righteous in Professor Dowden's Life of Shelley, if I had been justly dealt with.

During these six years I have been living a life of peaceful ignorance. I was not aware that Shelley's first wife was unfaithful to him, and that that was why he deserted her and wiped the stain from his sensitive honor by entering into soiled relations with Godwin's young daughter. This was all new to me when I heard it lately, and was told that the proofs of it were in this book, and that this book's verdict is accepted in the girls' colleges of America and its view taught in their literary classes.

In each of these six years multitudes of young people in our country have arrived at the Shelley-reading age. Are these six multitudes unacquainted with this life of Shelley? Perhaps they are; indeed, one may feel pretty sure that the great bulk of them are. To these, then, I address myself, in the hope that some account of this romantic historical fable and the fabulist's manner of constructing and adorning it may interest them.

First, as to its literary style. Our negroes in America have several ways of entertaining themselves which are not found among the whites anywhere. Among these inventions of theirs is one which is particularly popular with them. It is a competition in elegant deportment. They hire a hall and bank the spectators' seats in rising tiers along the two sides, leaving all the middle stretch of the floor free. A cake is provided as a prize for the winner in the competition, and a bench of experts in deportment is appointed to award it. Sometimes there are as many as fifty contestants, male and female, and five hundred spectators. One at a time the contestants enter, clothed regardless of expense in what each considers the perfection of style and taste, and walk down the vacant central space and back again with that multitude of critical eyes on them. All that the competitor knows of fine airs and graces he throws into his carriage, all that he knows of seductive expression he throws into his countenance. He may use all the helps he can devise: watch-chain to twirl with his fingers, cane to do graceful things with, snowy handkerchief to flourish and get artful effects out of, shiny new stovepipe hat to assist in his courtly bows; and the colored lady may have a fan to work up her effects with, and smile over and blush behind, and she may add other helps, according to her judgment. When the review by individual detail is over, a grand review of all the contestants in procession follows, with all the airs and graces and all the bowings and smirkings on exhibition at once, and this enables the bench of experts to make the necessary comparisons and arrive at a verdict. The successful competitor gets the prize which I have before mentioned, and an abundance of applause and envy along with it. The negroes have a name for this grave deportment-tournament; a name taken from the prize contended for. They call it a Cake-walk.

This Shelley biography is a literary cake-walk. The ordinary forms of speech are absent from it. All the pages, all the paragraphs, walk by sedately, elegantly, not to say mincingly, in their Sunday-best, shiny and sleek, perfumed, and with boutonnieres in their button-holes; it is rare to find even a chance sentence that has forgotten to dress. If the book wishes to tell us that Mary Godwin, child of sixteen, had known afflictions, the fact saunters forth in this nobby outfit: "Mary was herself not unlearned in the lore of pain"—meaning by that that she had not always traveled on asphalt; or, as some authorities would frame it, that she had "been there herself," a form which, while preferable to the book's form, is still not to be recommended. If the book wishes to tell us that Harriet Shelley hired a wet-nurse, that commonplace fact gets turned into a dancing-master, who does his professional bow before us in pumps and knee-breeches, with his fiddle under one arm and his crush-hat under the other, thus: "The beauty of Harriet's motherly relation to her babe was marred in Shelley's eyes by the introduction into his house of a hireling nurse to whom was delegated the mother's tenderest office."

This is perhaps the strangest book that has seen the light since Frankenstein. Indeed, it is a Frankenstein itself; a Frankenstein with the original infirmity supplemented by a new one; a Frankenstein with the reasoning faculty wanting. Yet it believes it can reason, and is always trying. It is not content to leave a mountain of fact standing in the clear sunshine, where the simplest reader can perceive its form, its details, and its relation to the rest of the landscape, but thinks it must help him examine it and understand it; so its drifting mind settles upon it with that intent, but always with one and the same result: there is a change of temperature and the mountain is hid in a fog. Every time it sets up a premise and starts to reason from it, there is a surprise in store for the reader. It is strangely nearsighted, cross-eyed, and purblind. Sometimes when a mastodon walks across the field of its vision it takes it for a rat; at other times it does not see it at all.

The materials of this biographical fable are facts, rumors, and poetry. They are connected together and harmonized by the help of suggestion, conjecture, innuendo, perversion, and semi-suppression.

The fable has a distinct object in view, but this object is not acknowledged in set words. Percy Bysshe Shelley has done something which in the case of other men is called a grave crime; it must be shown that in his case it is not that, because he does not think as other men do about these things.

Ought not that to be enough, if the fabulist is serious? Having proved that a crime is not a crime, was it worth while to go on and fasten the responsibility of a crime which was not a crime upon somebody else? What is the use of hunting down and holding to bitter account people who are responsible for other people's innocent acts?

Still, the fabulist thinks it a good idea to do that. In his view Shelley's first wife, Harriet, free of all offense as far as we have historical facts for guidance, must be held unforgivably responsible for her husband's innocent act in deserting her and taking up with another woman.

Any one will suspect that this task has its difficulties. Any one will divine that nice work is necessary here, cautious work, wily work, and that there is entertainment to be had in watching the magician do it. There is indeed entertainment in watching him. He arranges his facts, his rumors, and his poems on his table in full view of the house, and shows you that everything is there—no deception, everything fair and above board. And this is apparently true, yet there is a defect, for some of his best stock is hid in an appendix-basket behind the door, and you do not come upon it until the exhibition is over and the enchantment of your mind accomplished—as the magician thinks.

There is an insistent atmosphere of candor and fairness about this book which is engaging at first, then a little burdensome, then a trifle fatiguing, then progressively suspicious, annoying, irritating, and oppressive. It takes one some little time to find out that phrases which seem intended to guide the reader aright are there to mislead him; that phrases which seem intended to throw light are there to throw darkness; that phrases which seem intended to interpret a fact are there to misinterpret it; that phrases which seem intended to forestall prejudice are there to create it; that phrases which seem antidotes are poisons in disguise. The naked facts arrayed in the book establish Shelley's guilt in that one episode which disfigures his otherwise superlatively lofty and beautiful life; but the historian's careful and methodical misinterpretation of them transfers the responsibility to the wife's shoulders as he persuades himself. The few meager facts of Harriet Shelley's life, as furnished by the book, acquit her of offense; but by calling in the forbidden helps of rumor, gossip, conjecture, insinuation, and innuendo he destroys her character and rehabilitates Shelley's—as he believes. And in truth his unheroic work has not been barren of the results he aimed at; as witness the assertion made to me that girls in the colleges of America are taught that Harriet Shelley put a stain upon her husband's honor, and that that was what stung him into repurifying himself by deserting her and his child and entering into scandalous relations with a school-girl acquaintance of his.

If that assertion is true, they probably use a reduction of this work in those colleges, maybe only a sketch outlined from it. Such a thing as that could be harmful and misleading. They ought to cast it out and put the whole book in its place. It would not deceive. It would not deceive the janitor.

All of this book is interesting on account of the sorcerer's methods and the attractiveness of some of his characters and the repulsiveness of the rest, but no part of it is so much so as are the chapters wherein he tries to think he thinks he sets forth the causes which led to Shelley's desertion of his wife in 1814.

Harriet Westbrook was a school-girl sixteen years old. Shelley was teeming with advanced thought. He believed that Christianity was a degrading and selfish superstition, and he had a deep and sincere desire to rescue one of his sisters from it. Harriet was impressed by his various philosophies and looked upon him as an intellectual wonder—which indeed he was. He had an idea that she could give him valuable help in his scheme regarding his sister; therefore he asked her to correspond with him. She was quite willing. Shelley was not thinking of love, for he was just getting over a passion for his cousin, Harriet Grove, and just getting well steeped in one for Miss Hitchener, a school-teacher. What might happen to Harriet Westbrook before the letter-writing was ended did not enter his mind. Yet an older person could have made a good guess at it, for in person Shelley was as beautiful as an angel, he was frank, sweet, winning, unassuming, and so rich in unselfishness, generosities, and magnanimities that he made his whole generation seem poor in these great qualities by comparison. Besides, he was in distress. His college had expelled him for writing an atheistical pamphlet and afflicting the reverend heads of the university with it, his rich father and grandfather had closed their purses against him, his friends were cold. Necessarily, Harriet fell in love with him; and so deeply, indeed, that there was no way for Shelley to save her from suicide but to marry her. He believed himself to blame for this state of things, so the marriage took place. He was pretty fairly in love with Harriet, although he loved Miss Hitchener better. He wrote and explained the case to Miss Hitchener after the wedding, and he could not have been franker or more naive and less stirred up about the circumstance if the matter in issue had been a commercial transaction involving thirty-five dollars.

Shelley was nineteen. He was not a youth, but a man. He had never had any youth. He was an erratic and fantastic child during eighteen years, then he stepped into manhood, as one steps over a door-sill. He was curiously mature at nineteen in his ability to do independent thinking on the deep questions of life and to arrive at sharply definite decisions regarding them, and stick to them—stick to them and stand by them at cost of bread, friendships, esteem, respect, and approbation.

For the sake of his opinions he was willing to sacrifice all these valuable things, and did sacrifice them; and went on doing it, too, when he could at any moment have made himself rich and supplied himself with friends and esteem by compromising with his father, at the moderate expense of throwing overboard one or two indifferent details of his cargo of principles.

He and Harriet eloped to Scotland and got married. They took lodgings in Edinburgh of a sort answerable to their purse, which was about empty, and there their life was a happy, one and grew daily more so. They had only themselves for company, but they needed no additions to it. They were as cozy and contented as birds in a nest. Harriet sang evenings or read aloud; also she studied and tried to improve her mind, her husband instructing her in Latin. She was very beautiful, she was modest, quiet, genuine, and, according to her husband's testimony, she had no fine lady airs or aspirations about her. In Matthew Arnold's judgment, she was "a pleasing figure."

The pair remained five weeks in Edinburgh, and then took lodgings in York, where Shelley's college mate, Hogg, lived. Shelley presently ran down to London, and Hogg took this opportunity to make love to the young wife. She repulsed him, and reported the fact to her husband when he got back. It seems a pity that Shelley did not copy this creditable conduct of hers some time or other when under temptation, so that we might have seen the author of his biography hang the miracle in the skies and squirt rainbows at it.

At the end of the first year of marriage—the most trying year for any young couple, for then the mutual failings are coming one by one to light, and the necessary adjustments are being made in pain and tribulation—Shelley was able to recognize that his marriage venture had been a safe one. As we have seen, his love for his wife had begun in a rather shallow way and with not much force, but now it was become deep and strong, which entitles his wife to a broad credit mark, one may admit. He addresses a long and loving poem to her, in which both passion and worship appear:

Exhibit A

> "O thou
> 
> Whose dear love gleamed upon the gloomy path
> 
> Which this lone spirit travelled,
> 
> .............
> 
> ... wilt thou not turn
> 
> Those spirit-beaming eyes and look on me.
> 
> Until I be assured that Earth is Heaven
> 
> And Heaven is Earth?
> 
> ........
> 
> Harriet! let death all mortal ties dissolve,
> 
> But ours shall not be mortal."

Shelley also wrote a sonnet to her in August of this same year in celebration of her birthday:

Exhibit B

> "Ever as now with Love and Virtue's glow
> 
> May thy unwithering soul not cease to burn,
> 
> Still may thine heart with those pure thoughts o'erflow
> 
> Which force from mine such quick and warm return."

Was the girl of seventeen glad and proud and happy? We may conjecture that she was.

That was the year 1812. Another year passed still happily, still successfully—a child was born in June, 1813, and in September, three months later, Shelley addresses a poem to this child, Ianthe, in which he points out just when the little creature is most particularly dear to him:

Exhibit C

> "Dearest when most thy tender traits express

*The image of thy mother's loveliness."*

Up to this point the fabulist counsel for Shelley and prosecutor of his young wife has had easy sailing, but now his trouble begins, for Shelley is getting ready to make some unpleasant history for himself, and it will be necessary to put the blame of it on the wife.

Shelley had made the acquaintance of a charming gray-haired, young-hearted Mrs. Boinville, whose face "retained a certain youthful beauty"; she lived at Bracknell, and had a young daughter named Cornelia Turner, who was equipped with many fascinations. Apparently these people were sufficiently sentimental. Hogg says of Mrs. Boinville:

> *"The greater part of her associates were odious. I generally found there two or three sentimental young butchers, an eminently philosophical tinker, and several very unsophisticated medical practitioners or medical students, all of low origin and vulgar and offensive manners. They sighed, turned up their eyes, retailed philosophy, such as it was,"*
>
> *etc.*

Shelley moved to Bracknell, July 27th (this is still 1813) purposely to be near this unwholesome prairie-dogs' nest. The fabulist says: "It was the entrance into a world more amiable and exquisite than he had yet known."

"In this acquaintance the attraction was mutual"—and presently it grew to be very mutual indeed, between Shelley and Cornelia Turner, when they got to studying the Italian poets together. Shelley, "responding like a tremulous instrument to every breath of passion or of sentiment," had his chance here. It took only four days for Cornelia's attractions to begin to dim Harriet's. Shelley arrived on the 27th of July; on the 31st he wrote a sonnet to Harriet in which "one detects already the little rift in the lover's lute which had seemed to be healed or never to have gaped at all when the later and happier sonnet to Ianthe was written"—in September, we remember:

Exhibit D

*"EVENING. TO HARRIET*

*"O thou bright Sun! Beneath the dark blue line*

*Of western distance that sublime descendest,*

*And, gleaming lovelier as thy beams decline,*

*Thy million hues to every vapor lendest,*

*And over cobweb, lawn, and grove, and stream*

*Sheddest the liquid magic of thy light,*

*Till calm Earth, with the parting splendor bright,*

*Shows like the vision of a beauteous dream;*

*What gazer now with astronomic eye*

*Could coldly count the spots within thy sphere?*

*Such were thy lover, Harriet, could he fly*

*The thoughts of all that makes his passion dear,*

*And turning senseless from thy warm caress*

*Pick flaws in our close-woven happiness."*

I cannot find the "rift"; still it may be there. What the poem seems to say is, that a person would be coldly ungrateful who could consent to count and consider little spots and flaws in such a warm, great, satisfying sun as Harriet is. It is a "little rift which had seemed to be healed, or never to have gaped at all." That is, "one detects" a little rift which perhaps had never existed. How does one do that? How does one see the invisible? It is the fabulist's secret; he knows how to detect what does not exist, he knows how to see what is not seeable; it is his gift, and he works it many a time to poor dead Harriet Shelley's deep damage.

"As yet, however, if there was a speck upon Shelley's happiness it was no more than a speck"—meaning the one which one detects where "it may never have gaped at all"—"nor had Harriet cause for discontent."

Shelley's Latin instructions to his wife had ceased. "From a teacher he had now become a pupil." Mrs. Boinville and her young married daughter Cornelia were teaching him Italian poetry; a fact which warns one to receive with some caution that other statement that Harriet had no "cause for discontent."

Shelley had stopped instructing Harriet in Latin, as before mentioned. The biographer thinks that the busy life in London some time back, and the intrusion of the baby, account for this. These were hindrances, but were there no others? He is always overlooking a detail here and there that might be valuable in helping us understand a situation. For instance, when a man has been hard at work at the Italian poets with a pretty woman, hour after hour, and responding like a tremulous instrument to every breath of passion or of sentiment in the meantime, that man is dog-tired when he gets home, and he can't teach his wife Latin; it would be unreasonable to expect it.

Up to this time we have submitted to having Mrs. Boinville pushed upon us as ostensibly concerned in these Italian lessons, but the biographer drops her now, of his own accord. Cornelia "perhaps" is sole teacher. Hogg says she was a prey to a kind of sweet melancholy, arising from causes purely imaginary; she required consolation, and found it in Petrarch. He also says, "Bysshe entered at once fully into her views and caught the soft infection, breathing the tenderest and sweetest melancholy, as every true poet ought."

Then the author of the book interlards a most stately and fine compliment to Cornelia, furnished by a man of approved judgment who knew her well "in later years." It is a very good compliment indeed, and she no doubt deserved it in her "later years," when she had for generations ceased to be sentimental and lackadaisical, and was no longer engaged in enchanting young husbands and sowing sorrow for young wives. But why is that compliment to that old gentlewoman intruded there? Is it to make the reader believe she was well-chosen and safe society for a young, sentimental husband? The biographer's device was not well planned. That old person was not present—it was her other self that was there, her young, sentimental, melancholy, warm-blooded self, in those early sweet times before antiquity had cooled her off and mossed her back.

"In choosing for friends such women as Mrs. Newton, Mrs. Boinville, and Cornelia Turner, Shelley gave good proof of his insight and discrimination." That is the fabulist's opinion—Harriet Shelley's is not reported.

Early in August, Shelley was in London trying to raise money. In September he wrote the poem to the baby, already quoted from. In the first week of October Shelley and family went to Warwick, then to Edinburgh, arriving there about the middle of the month.

"Harriet was happy." Why? The author furnishes a reason, but hides from us whether it is history or conjecture; it is because "the babe had borne the journey well." It has all the aspect of one of his artful devices—flung in in his favorite casual way—the way he has when he wants to draw one's attention away from an obvious thing and amuse it with some trifle that is less obvious but more useful—in a history like this. The obvious thing is, that Harriet was happy because there was much territory between her husband and Cornelia Turner now; and because the perilous Italian lessons were taking a rest; and because, if there chanced to be any respondings like a tremulous instrument to every breath of passion or of sentiment in stock in these days, she might hope to get a share of them herself; and because, with her husband liberated, now, from the fetid fascinations of that sentimental retreat so pitilessly described by Hogg, who also dubbed it "Shelley's paradise" later, she might hope to persuade him to stay away from it permanently; and because she might also hope that his brain would cool, now, and his heart become healthy, and both brain and heart consider the situation and resolve that it would be a right and manly thing to stand by this girl-wife and her child and see that they were honorably dealt with, and cherished and protected and loved by the man that had promised these things, and so be made happy and kept so. And because, also—may we conjecture this?—we may hope for the privilege of taking up our cozy Latin lessons again, that used to be so pleasant, and brought us so near together—so near, indeed, that often our heads touched, just as heads do over Italian lessons; and our hands met in casual and unintentional, but still most delicious and thrilling little contacts and momentary clasps, just as they inevitably do over Italian lessons. Suppose one should say to any young wife: "I find that your husband is poring over the Italian poets and being instructed in the beautiful Italian language by the lovely Cornelia Robinson"—would that cozy picture fail to rise before her mind? would its possibilities fail to suggest themselves to her? would there be a pang in her heart and a blush on her face? or, on the contrary, would the remark give her pleasure, make her joyous and gay? Why, one needs only to make the experiment—the result will not be uncertain.

However, we learn—by authority of deeply reasoned and searching conjecture—that the baby bore the journey well, and that that was why the young wife was happy. That accounts for two per cent. of the happiness, but it was not right to imply that it accounted for the other ninety-eight also.

Peacock, a scholar, poet, and friend of the Shelleys, was of their party when they went away. He used to laugh at the Boinville menagerie, and "was not a favorite." One of the Boinville group, writing to Hogg, said, "The Shelleys have made an addition to their party in the person of a cold scholar, who, I think, has neither taste nor feeling. This, Shelley will perceive sooner or later, for his warm nature craves sympathy." True, and Shelley will fight his way back there to get it—there will be no way to head him off.

Toward the end of November it was necessary for Shelley to pay a business visit to London, and he conceived the project of leaving Harriet and the baby in Edinburgh with Harriet's sister, Eliza Westbrook, a sensible, practical maiden lady about thirty years old, who had spent a great part of her time with the family since the marriage. She was an estimable woman, and Shelley had had reason to like her, and did like her; but along about this time his feeling towards her changed. Part of Shelley's plan, as he wrote Hogg, was to spend his London evenings with the Newtons—members of the Boinville Hysterical Society. But, alas, when he arrived early in December, that pleasant game was partially blocked, for Eliza and the family arrived with him. We are left destitute of conjectures at this point by the biographer, and it is my duty to supply one. I chance the conjecture that it was Eliza who interfered with that game. I think she tried to do what she could towards modifying the Boinville connection, in the interest of her young sister's peace and honor.

If it was she who blocked that game, she was not strong enough to block the next one. Before the month and year were out—no date given, let us call it Christmas—Shelley and family were nested in a furnished house in Windsor, "at no great distance from the Boinvilles"—these decoys still residing at Bracknell.

What we need, now, is a misleading conjecture. We get it with characteristic promptness and depravity:

> *"But Prince Athanase found not the aged Zonoras, the friend of*
>
> *his boyhood, in any wanderings to Windsor. Dr. Lind had died*
>
> *a year since, and with his death Windsor must have lost, for*
>
> *Shelley, its chief attraction."*

Still, not to mention Shelley's wife, there was Bracknell, at any rate. While Bracknell remains, all solace is not lost. Shelley is represented by this biographer as doing a great many careless things, but to my mind this hiring a furnished house for three months in order to be with a man who has been dead a year, is the carelessest of them all. One feels for him—that is but natural, and does us honor besides—yet one is vexed, for all that. He could have written and asked about the aged Zonoras before taking the house. He may not have had the address, but that is nothing—any postman would know the aged Zonoras; a dead postman would remember a name like that.

And yet, why throw a rag like this to us ravening wolves? Is it seriously supposable that we will stop to chew it and let our prey escape? No, we are getting to expect this kind of device, and to give it merely a sniff for certainty's sake and then walk around it and leave it lying. Shelley was not after the aged Zonoras; he was pointed for Cornelia and the Italian lessons, for his warm nature was craving sympathy.

## II

The year 1813 is just ended now, and we step into 1814.

To recapitulate, how much of Cornelia's society has Shelley had, thus far? Portions of August and September, and four days of July. That is to say, he has had opportunity to enjoy it, more or less, during that brief period. Did he want some more of it? We must fall back upon history, and then go to conjecturing.

> *"In the early part of the year 1814, Shelley was a frequent visitor at Bracknell."*

"Frequent" is a cautious word, in this author's mouth; the very cautiousness of it, the vagueness of it, provokes suspicion; it makes one suspect that this frequency was more frequent than the mere common everyday kinds of frequency which one is in the habit of averaging up with the unassuming term "frequent." I think so because they fixed up a bedroom for him in the Boinville house. One doesn't need a bedroom if one is only going to run over now and then in a disconnected way to respond like a tremulous instrument to every breath of passion or of sentiment and rub up one's Italian poetry a little.

The young wife was not invited, perhaps. If she was, she most certainly did not come, or she would have straightened the room up; the most ignorant of us knows that a wife would not endure a room in the condition in which Hogg found this one when he occupied it one night. Shelley was away—why, nobody can divine. Clothes were scattered about, there were books on every side: "Wherever a book could be laid was an open book turned down on its face to keep its place." It seems plain that the wife was not invited. No, not that; I think she was invited, but said to herself that she could not bear to go there and see another young woman touching heads with her husband over an Italian book and making thrilling hand-contacts with him accidentally.

As remarked, he was a frequent visitor there, "where he found an easeful resting-place in the house of Mrs. Boinville—the white-haired Maimuna—and of her daughter, Mrs. Turner." The aged Zonoras was deceased, but the white-haired Maimuna was still on deck, as we see. "Three charming ladies entertained the mocker (Hogg) with cups of tea, late hours, Wieland's Agathon, sighs and smiles, and the celestial manna of refined sentiment."

"Such," says Hogg, "were the delights of Shelley's paradise in Bracknell."

The white-haired Maimuna presently writes to Hogg:

> *"I will not have you despise home-spun pleasures. Shelley is making a trial of them with us—"*

A trial of them. It may be called that. It was March 11, and he had been in the house a month. She continues:

> Shelley *"likes them so well that he is resolved to leave off rambling—"*

But he has already left it off. He has been there a month.

> *"And begin a course of them himself."*

But he has already begun it. He has been at it a month. He likes it so well that he has forgotten all about his wife, as a letter of his reveals.

> *"Seriously, I think his mind and body want rest."*

Yet he has been resting both for a month, with Italian, and tea, and manna of sentiment, and late hours, and every restful thing a young husband could need for the refreshment of weary limbs and a sore conscience, and a nagging sense of shabbiness and treachery.

> *"His journeys after what he has never found have racked his purse and his tranquillity. He is resolved to take a little care of the former, in pity to the latter, which I applaud, and shall second with all my might."*

But she does not say whether the young wife, a stranger and lonely yonder, wants another woman and her daughter Cornelia to be lavishing so much inflamed interest on her husband or not. That young wife is always silent—we are never allowed to hear from her. She must have opinions about such things, she cannot be indifferent, she must be approving or disapproving, surely she would speak if she were allowed—even to-day and from her grave she would, if she could, I think—but we get only the other side, they keep her silent always.

> "He has deeply interested us. In the course of your intimacy
>
> he must have made you feel what we now feel for him. He is
>
> seeking a house close to us—"

Ah! he is not close enough yet, it seems—

> "and if he succeeds we shall have an additional motive to
>
> induce you to come among us in the summer."

The reader would puzzle a long time and not guess the biographer's comment upon the above letter. It is this:

> "These sound like words of A considerate and judicious friend."

That is what he thinks. That is, it is what he thinks he thinks. No, that is not quite it: it is what he thinks he can stupefy a particularly and unspeakably dull reader into thinking it is what he thinks. He makes that comment with the knowledge that Shelley is in love with this woman's daughter, and that it is because of the fascinations of these two that Shelley has deserted his wife—for this month, considering all the circumstances, and his new passion, and his employment of the time, amounted to desertion; that is its rightful name. We cannot know how the wife regarded it and felt about it; but if she could have read the letter which Shelley was writing to Hogg four or five days later, we could guess her thought and how she felt. Hear him:.......

> "I have been staying with Mrs. Boinville for the last month;
>
> I have escaped, in the society of all that philosophy and
>
> friendship combine, from the dismaying solitude of myself."

It is fair to conjecture that he was feeling ashamed.

> "They have revived in my heart the expiring flame of life. I have felt myself translated to a paradise which has nothing of mortality but its transitoriness; my heart sickens at the view of that necessity which will quickly divide me from the delightful tranquillity of this happy home—for it has become my home.
>
> .......
>
> "Eliza is still with us—not here!—but will be with me when the infinite malice of destiny forces me to depart."

Eliza is she who blocked that game—the game in London—the one where we were purposing to dine every night with one of the "three charming ladies" who fed tea and manna and late hours to Hogg at Bracknell.

Shelley could send Eliza away, of course; could have cleared her out long ago if so minded, just as he had previously done with a predecessor of hers whom he had first worshiped and then turned against; but perhaps she was useful there as a thin excuse for staying away himself.

> "I am now but little inclined to contest this point. I certainly hate her with all my heart and soul....
>
> "It is a sight which awakens an inexpressible sensation of disgust and horror, to see her caress my poor little Ianthe, in whom I may hereafter find the consolation of sympathy. I sometimes feel faint with the fatigue of checking the overflowings of my unbounded abhorrence for this miserable wretch. But she is no more than a blind and loathsome worm, that cannot see to sting.

"I have begun to learn Italian again.... Cornelia assists me in this language. Did I not once tell you that I thought her cold and reserved? She is the reverse of this, as she is the reverse of everything bad. She inherits all the divinity of her mother.... I have sometimes forgotten that I am not an inmate of this delightful home—that a time will come which will cast me again into the boundless ocean of abhorred society.

"I have written nothing but one stanza, which has no meaning, and that I have only written in thought:

> "Thy dewy looks sink in my breast;
> Thy gentle words stir poison there;
> Thou hast disturbed the only rest
> That was the portion of despair.
> Subdued to duty's hard control,
> I could have borne my wayward lot:
> The chains that bind this rained soul
> Had cankered then, but crushed it not.

"This is the vision of a delirious and distempered dream, which passes away at the cold clear light of morning. Its surpassing excellence and exquisite perfections have no more reality than *the color of an autumnal sunset."*

Then it did not refer to his wife. That is plain; otherwise he would have said so. It is well that he explained that it has no meaning, for if he had not done that, the previous soft references to Cornelia and the way he has come to feel about her now would make us think she was the person who had inspired it while teaching him how to read the warm and ruddy Italian poets during a month.

The biography observes that portions of this letter "read like the tired moaning of a wounded creature." Guesses at the nature of the wound are permissible; we will hazard one.

Read by the light of Shelley's previous history, his letter seems to be the cry of a tortured conscience. Until this time it was a conscience that had never felt a pang or known a smirch. It was the conscience of one who, until this time, had never done a dishonorable thing, or an ungenerous, or cruel, or treacherous thing, but was now doing all of these, and was keenly aware of it. Up to this time Shelley had been master of his nature, and it was a nature which was as beautiful and as nearly perfect as any merely human nature may be. But he was drunk now, with a debasing passion, and was not himself. There is nothing in his previous history that is in character with the Shelley of this letter. He had done boyish things, foolish things, even crazy things, but never a thing to be ashamed of. He had done things which one might laugh at, but the privilege of laughing was limited always to the thing itself; you could not laugh at the motive back of it—that was high, that was noble. His most fantastic and quixotic acts had a purpose back of them which made them fine, often great, and made the rising laugh seem profanation and quenched it; quenched it, and changed the impulse to homage.

Up to this time he had been loyalty itself, where his obligations lay—treachery was new to him; he had never done an ignoble thing—baseness was new to him; he had never done an unkind thing—that also was new to him.

This was the author of that letter, this was the man who had deserted his young wife and was lamenting, because he must leave another woman's house which had become a "home" to him, and go away. Is he lamenting mainly because he must go back to his wife and child? No, the lament is mainly for what he is to leave behind him. The physical comforts of the house? No, in his life he had never attached importance to such things. Then the thing which he grieves to leave is narrowed down to a person—to the person whose "dewy looks" had sunk into his breast, and whose seducing words had "stirred poison there."

He was ashamed of himself, his conscience was upbraiding him. He was the slave of a degrading love; he was drunk with his passion, the real Shelley was in temporary eclipse. This is the verdict which his previous history must certainly deliver upon this episode, I think.

One must be allowed to assist himself with conjectures like these when trying to find his way through a literary swamp which has so many misleading finger-boards up as this book is furnished with.

We have now arrived at a part of the swamp where the difficulties and perplexities are going to be greater than any we have yet met with—where, indeed, the finger-boards are multitudinous, and the most of them pointing diligently in the wrong direction. We are to be told by the biography why Shelley deserted his wife and child and took up with Cornelia Turner and Italian. It was not on account of Cornelia's sighs and sentimentalities and tea and manna and late hours and soft and sweet and industrious enticements; no, it was because "his happiness in his home had been wounded and bruised almost to death."

It had been wounded and bruised almost to death in this way:

1st. Harriet persuaded him to set up a carriage.

2d. After the intrusion of the baby, Harriet stopped reading aloud and studying.

3d. Harriet's walks with Hogg "commonly conducted us to some fashionable bonnet-shop."

4th. Harriet hired a wet-nurse.

5th. When an operation was being performed upon the baby, "Harriet stood by, narrowly observing all that was done, but, to the astonishment of the operator, betraying not the smallest sign of emotion."

6th. Eliza Westbrook, sister-in-law, was still of the household.

The evidence against Harriet Shelley is all in; there is no more. Upon these six counts she stands indicted of the crime of driving her husband into that sty at Bracknell; and this crime, by these helps, the biographical prosecuting attorney has set himself the task of proving upon her.

Does the biographer call himself the attorney for the prosecution? No, only to himself, privately; publicly he is the passionless, disinterested, impartial judge on the bench. He holds up his judicial scales before the world, that all may see; and it all tries to look so fair that a blind person would sometimes fail to see him slip the false weights in.

Shelley's happiness in his home had been wounded and bruised almost to death, first, because Harriet had persuaded him to set up a carriage. I cannot discover that any evidence is offered that she asked him to set up a carriage. Still, if she did, was it a heavy offense? Was it unique? Other young wives had committed it before, others have committed it since. Shelley had dearly loved her in those London days; possibly he set up the carriage gladly to please her; affectionate young husbands do such things. When Shelley ran away with another girl, by-and-by, this girl persuaded him to pour the price of many carriages and many horses down the bottomless well of her father's debts, but this impartial judge finds no fault with that. Once she appeals to Shelley to raise money—necessarily by borrowing, there was no other way—to pay her father's debts with at a time when Shelley was in danger of being arrested and imprisoned for his own debts; yet the good judge finds no fault with her even for this.

First and last, Shelley emptied into that rapacious mendicant's lap a sum which cost him—for he borrowed it at ruinous rates—from eighty to one hundred thousand dollars. But it was Mary Godwin's papa, the supplications were often sent through Mary, the good judge is Mary's strenuous friend, so Mary gets no censures. On the Continent Mary rode in her private carriage, built, as Shelley boasts, "by one of the best makers in Bond Street," yet the good judge makes not even a passing comment on this iniquity. Let us throw out Count No. 1 against Harriet Shelley as being far-fetched, and frivolous.

Shelley's happiness in his home had been wounded and bruised almost to death, secondly, because Harriet's studies "had dwindled away to nothing, Bysshe had ceased to express any interest in them." At what time was this? It was when Harriet "had fully recovered from the fatigue of her first effort of maternity... and was now in full force, vigor, and effect." Very well, the baby was born two days before the close of June. It took the mother a month to get back her full force, vigor, and effect; this brings us to July 27th and the deadly Cornelia. If a wife of eighteen is studying with her husband and he gets smitten with another woman, isn't he likely to lose interest in his wife's studies for that reason, and is not his wife's interest in her studies likely to languish for the same reason? Would not the mere sight of those books of hers sharpen the pain that is in her heart? This sudden breaking down of a mutual intellectual interest of two years' standing is coincident with Shelley's re-encounter with Cornelia; and we are allowed to gather from that time forth for nearly two months he did all his studying in that person's society. We feel at liberty to rule out Count No. 2 from the indictment against Harriet.

Shelley's happiness in his home had been wounded and bruised almost to death, thirdly, because Harriet's walks with Hogg commonly led to some fashionable bonnet-shop. I offer no palliation; I only ask why the dispassionate, impartial judge did not offer one himself—merely, I mean, to offset his leniency in a similar case or two where the girl who ran away with Harriet's husband was the shopper. There are several occasions where she interested herself with shopping—among them being walks which ended at the bonnet-shop—yet in none of these cases does she get a word of blame from the good judge, while in one of them he covers the deed with a justifying remark, she doing the shopping that time to find easement for her mind, her child having died.

Shelley's happiness in his home had been wounded and bruised almost to death, fourthly, by the introduction there of a wet-nurse. The wet-nurse was introduced at the time of the Edinburgh sojourn, immediately after Shelley had been enjoying the two months of study with Cornelia which broke up his wife's studies and destroyed his personal interest in them. Why, by this time, nothing that Shelley's wife could do would have been satisfactory to him, for he was in love with another woman, and was never going to be contented again until he got back to her. If he had been still in love with his wife it is not easily conceivable that he would care much who nursed the baby, provided the baby was well nursed. Harriet's jealousy was assuredly voicing itself now, Shelley's conscience was assuredly nagging him, pestering him, persecuting him. Shelley needed excuses for his altered attitude toward his wife; Providence pitied him and sent the wet-nurse. If Providence had sent him a cotton doughnut it would have answered just as well; all he wanted was something to find fault with.

Shelley's happiness in his home had been wounded and bruised almost to death, fifthly, because Harriet narrowly watched a surgical operation which was being performed upon her child, and, "to the astonishment of the operator," who was watching Harriet instead of attending to his operation, she betrayed "not the smallest sign of emotion." The author of this biography was not ashamed to set down that exultant slander. He was apparently not aware that it was a small business to bring into his court a witness whose name he does not know, and whose character and veracity there is none to vouch for, and allow him to strike this blow at the mother-heart of this friendless girl. The biographer says, "We may not infer from this that Harriet did not feel"—why put it in, then?—"but we learn that those about her could believe her to be hard and insensible." Who were those who were about her? Her husband? He hated her now, because he was in love elsewhere. Her sister? Of course that is not charged. Peacock? Peacock does not testify. The wet-nurse? She does not testify. If any others were there we have no mention of them. "Those about her" are reduced to one person—her husband. Who reports the circumstance? It is Hogg. Perhaps he was there—we do not know. But if he was, he still got his information at second-hand, as it was the operator who noticed Harriet's lack of emotion, not himself. Hogg is not given to saying kind things when Harriet is his subject. He may have said them the time that he tried to tempt her to soil her honor, but after that he mentions her usually with a sneer. "Among those who were about her" was one witness well equipped to silence all tongues, abolish all doubts, set our minds at rest; one witness, not called, and not callable, whose evidence, if we could but get it, would outweigh the oaths of whole battalions of hostile Hoggs and nameless surgeons—the baby. I wish we had the baby's testimony; and yet if we had it it would not do us any good—a furtive conjecture, a sly insinuation, a pious "if" or two, would be smuggled in, here and there, with a solemn air of judicial investigation, and its positiveness would wilt into dubiety.

The biographer says of Harriet, "If words of tender affection and motherly pride proved the reality of love, then undoubtedly she loved her firstborn child." That is, if mere empty words can prove it, it stands proved—and in this way, without committing himself, he gives the reader a chance to infer that there isn't any extant evidence but words, and that he doesn't take much stock in them. How seldom he shows his hand! He is always lurking behind a non-committal "if" or something of that kind; always gliding and dodging around, distributing colorless poison here and there and everywhere, but always leaving himself in a position to say that his language will be found innocuous if taken to pieces and examined. He clearly exhibits a steady and never-relaxing purpose to make Harriet the scapegoat for her husband's first great sin—but it is in the general view that this is revealed, not in the details. His insidious literature is like blue water; you know what it is that makes it blue, but you cannot produce and verify any detail of the cloud of microscopic dust in it that does it. Your adversary can dip up a glassful and show you that it is pure white and you cannot deny it; and he can dip the lake dry, glass by glass, and show that every glassful is white, and prove it to any one's eye—and yet that lake was blue and you can swear it. This book is blue—with slander in solution.

Let the reader examine, for example, the paragraph of comment which immediately follows the letter containing Shelley's self-exposure which we have been considering. This is it. One should inspect the individual sentences as they go by, then pass them in procession and review the cake-walk as a whole:

> *"Shelley's happiness in his home, as is evident from this pathetic letter, had been fatally stricken; it is evident,*

> also, that he knew where duty lay; he felt that his part was to take up his burden, silently and sorrowfully, and to bear it henceforth with the quietness of despair. But we can perceive that he scarcely possessed the strength and fortitude needful for success in such an attempt. And clearly Shelley himself was aware how perilous it was to accept that respite of blissful ease which he enjoyed in the Boinville household; for gentle voices and dewy looks and words of sympathy could not fail to remind him of an ideal of tranquillity or of joy which could never be his, and which he must henceforth sternly exclude from his imagination."

That paragraph commits the author in no way. Taken sentence by sentence it asserts nothing against anybody or in favor of anybody, pleads for nobody, accuses nobody. Taken detail by detail, it is as innocent as moonshine. And yet, taken as a whole, it is a design against the reader; its intent is to remove the feeling which the letter must leave with him if let alone, and put a different one in its place—to remove a feeling justified by the letter and substitute one not justified by it. The letter itself gives you no uncertain picture—no lecturer is needed to stand by with a stick and point out its details and let on to explain what they mean. The picture is the very clear and remorsefully faithful picture of a fallen and fettered angel who is ashamed of himself; an angel who beats his soiled wings and cries, who complains to the woman who enticed him that he could have borne his wayward lot, he could have stood by his duty if it had not been for her beguilements; an angel who rails at the "boundless ocean of abhorred society," and rages at his poor judicious sister-in-law. If there is any dignity about this spectacle it will escape most people.

Yet when the paragraph of comment is taken as a whole, the picture is full of dignity and pathos; we have before us a blameless and noble spirit stricken to the earth by malign powers, but not conquered; tempted, but grandly putting the temptation away; enmeshed by subtle coils, but sternly resolved to rend them and march forth victorious, at any peril of life or limb. Curtain—slow music.

Was it the purpose of the paragraph to take the bad taste of Shelley's letter out of the reader's mouth? If that was not it, good ink was wasted; without that, it has no relevancy—the multiplication table would have padded the space as rationally.

We have inspected the six reasons which we are asked to believe drove a man of conspicuous patience, honor, justice, fairness, kindliness, and iron firmness, resolution, and steadfastness, from the wife whom he loved and who loved him, to a refuge in the mephitic paradise of Bracknell. These are six infinitely little reasons; but there were six colossal ones, and these the counsel for the destruction of Harriet Shelley persists in not considering very important.

Moreover, the colossal six preceded the little six and had done the mischief before they were born. Let us double-column the twelve; then we shall see at a glance that each little reason is in turn answered by a retorting reason of a size to overshadow it and make it insignificant:

| | |
|---|---|
| *1. Harriet sets up carriage.* | *1. CORNELIA TURNER.* |
| *2. Harriet stops studying.* | *2. CORNELIA TURNER.* |
| *3. Harriet goes to bonnet-shop.* | *3. CORNELIA TURNER.* |
| *4. Harriet takes a wet-nurse.* | *4. CORNELIA TURNER.* |
| *5. Harriet has too much nerve.* | *5. CORNELIA TURNER.* |
| *6. Detested sister-in-law* | *6. CORNELIA TURNER.* |

As soon as we comprehend that Cornelia Turner and the Italian lessons happened before the little six had been discovered to be grievances, we understand why Shelley's happiness in his home had been wounded and bruised almost to death, and no one can persuade us into laying it on Harriet. Shelley and Cornelia are the responsible persons, and we cannot in honor and decency allow the cruelties which they practised upon the unoffending wife to be pushed aside in order to give us a chance to waste time and tears over six sentimental justifications of an offense which the six can't justify, nor even respectably assist in justifying.

Six? There were seven; but in charity to the biographer the seventh ought not to be exposed. Still, he hung it out himself, and not only hung it out, but thought it was a good point in Shelley's favor. For two years Shelley found sympathy and intellectual food and all that at home; there was enough for spiritual and mental support, but not enough for luxury; and so, at the end of the contented two years, this latter detail justifies him in going bag and baggage over to Cornelia Turner and supplying the rest of his need in the way of surplus sympathy and intellectual pie unlawfully. By the same reasoning a man in merely comfortable circumstances may rob a bank without sin.

## III

It is 1814, it is the 16th of March, Shelley has written his letter, he has been in the Boinville paradise a month, his deserted wife is in her husbandless home. Mischief had been wrought. It is the biographer who concedes this. We greatly need some light on Harriet's side of the case now; we need to know how she enjoyed the month, but there is no way to inform ourselves; there seems to be a strange absence of documents and letters and diaries on that side. Shelley kept a diary, the approaching Mary Godwin kept a diary, her father kept one, her half-sister by marriage, adoption, and the dispensation of God kept one, and the entire tribe and all its friends wrote and received letters, and the letters were kept and are producible when this biography needs them; but there are only three or four scraps of Harriet's writing, and no diary. Harriet wrote plenty of letters to her husband—nobody knows where they are, I suppose; she wrote plenty of letters to other people—apparently they have disappeared, too. Peacock says she wrote good letters, but apparently interested people had sagacity enough to mislay them in time. After all her industry she went down into her grave and lies silent there—silent, when she has so much need to speak. We can only wonder at this mystery, not account for it.

No, there is no way of finding out what Harriet's state of feeling was during the month that Shelley was disporting himself in the Bracknell paradise. We have to fall back upon conjecture, as our fabulist does when he has nothing more substantial to work with. Then we easily conjecture that as the days dragged by Harriet's heart grew heavier and heavier under its two burdens—shame and resentment: the shame of being pointed at and gossiped about as a deserted wife, and resentment against the woman who had beguiled her husband from her and now kept him in a disreputable captivity. Deserted wives—deserted whether for cause or without cause—find small charity among the virtuous and the discreet. We conjecture that one after another the neighbors ceased to call; that one after another they got to being "engaged" when Harriet called; that finally they one after the other cut her dead on the street; that after that she stayed in the house daytimes, and brooded over her sorrows, and nighttimes did the same, there being nothing else to do with the heavy hours and the silence and solitude and the dreary intervals which sleep should have charitably bridged, but didn't.

Yes, mischief had been wrought. The biographer arrives at this conclusion, and it is a most just one. Then, just as you begin to half hope he is going to discover the cause of it and launch hot bolts of wrath at the guilty manufacturers of it, you have to turn away disappointed. You are disappointed, and you sigh. This is what he says —the italics ["] are mine:

> *"However the mischief may have been wrought—'and at this day no one can wish to heap blame on any buried head'—"*

So it is poor Harriet, after all. Stern justice must take its course—justice tempered with delicacy, justice tempered with compassion, justice that pities a forlorn dead girl and refuses to strike her. Except in the back. Will not be ignoble and say the harsh thing, but only insinuate it. Stern justice knows about the carriage and the wet-nurse and the bonnet-shop and the other dark things that caused this sad mischief, and may not, must not blink them; so it delivers judgment where judgment belongs, but softens the blow by not seeming to deliver judgment at all. To resume—the italics are mine:

> *"However the mischief may have been wrought—and at this day no one can wish to heap blame on any buried head—'it is certain that some cause or causes of deep division between Shelley and his wife were in operation during the early part of the year 1814'."*

This shows penetration. No deduction could be more accurate than this. There were indeed some causes of deep division. But next comes another disappointing sentence:

> *"To guess at the precise nature of these causes, in the absence*

*of definite statement, were useless."*

Why, he has already been guessing at them for several pages, and we have been trying to outguess him, and now all of a sudden he is tired of it and won't play any more. It is not quite fair to us. However, he will get over this by-and-by, when Shelley commits his next indiscretion and has to be guessed out of it at Harriet's expense.

"We may rest content with Shelley's own words"—in a Chancery paper drawn up by him three years later. They were these: "Delicacy forbids me to say more than that we were disunited by incurable dissensions."

As for me, I do not quite see why we should rest content with anything of the sort. It is not a very definite statement. It does not necessarily mean anything more than that he did not wish to go into the tedious details of those family quarrels. Delicacy could quite properly excuse him from saying, "I was in love with Cornelia all that time; my wife kept crying and worrying about it and upbraiding me and begging me to cut myself free from a connection which was wronging her and disgracing us both; and I being stung by these reproaches retorted with fierce and bitter speeches—for it is my nature to do that when I am stirred, especially if the target of them is a person whom I had greatly loved and respected before, as witness my various attitudes towards Miss Hitchener, the Gisbornes, Harriet's sister, and others—and finally I did not improve this state of things when I deserted my wife and spent a whole month with the woman who had infatuated me."

No, he could not go into those details, and we excuse him; but, nevertheless, we do not rest content with this bland proposition to puff away that whole long disreputable episode with a single mean, meaningless remark of Shelley's.

We do admit that "it is certain that some cause or causes of deep division were in operation." We would admit it just the same if the grammar of the statement were as straight as a string, for we drift into pretty indifferent grammar ourselves when we are absorbed in historical work; but we have to decline to admit that we cannot guess those cause or causes.

But guessing is not really necessary. There is evidence attainable—evidence from the batch discredited by the biographer and set out at the back door in his appendix-basket; and yet a court of law would think twice before throwing it out, whereas it would be a hardy person who would venture to offer in such a place a good part of the material which is placed before the readers of this book as "evidence," and so treated by this daring biographer. Among some letters (in the appendix-basket) from Mrs. Godwin, detailing the Godwinian share in the Shelleyan events of 1814, she tells how Harriet Shelley came to her and her husband, agitated and weeping, to implore them to forbid Shelley the house, and prevent his seeing Mary Godwin.

> "She related that last November he had fallen in love with Mrs. Turner and paid her such marked attentions Mr. Turner, the husband, had carried off his wife to Devonshire."

The biographer finds a technical fault in this; "the Shelleys were in Edinburgh in November." What of that? The woman is recalling a conversation which is more than two months old; besides, she was probably more intent upon the central and important fact of it than upon its unimportant date. Harriet's quoted statement has some sense in it; for that reason, if for no other, it ought to have been put in the body of the book. Still, that would not have answered; even the biographer's enemy could not be cruel enough to ask him to let this real grievance, this compact and substantial and picturesque figure, this rawhead-and-bloody-bones, come striding in there among those pale shams, those rickety specters labeled WET-NURSE, BONNET-SHOP, and so on—no, the father of all malice could not ask the biographer to expose his pathetic goblins to a competition like that.

The fabulist finds fault with the statement because it has a technical error in it; and he does this at the moment that he is furnishing us an error himself, and of a graver sort. He says:

> "If Turner carried off his wife to Devonshire he brought her back and Shelley was staying with her and her mother on terms

*of cordial intimacy in March, 1814."*

We accept the "cordial intimacy"—it was the very thing Harriet was complaining of—but there is nothing to show that it was Turner who brought his wife back. The statement is thrown in as if it were not only true, but was proof that Turner was not uneasy. Turner's movements are proof of nothing. Nothing but a statement from Turner's mouth would have any value here, and he made none.

Six days after writing his letter Shelley and his wife were together again for a moment—to get remarried according to the rites of the English Church.

Within three weeks the new husband and wife were apart again, and the former was back in his odorous paradise. This time it is the wife who does the deserting. She finds Cornelia too strong for her, probably. At any rate, she goes away with her baby and sister, and we have a playful fling at her from good Mrs. Boinville, the "mysterious spinner Maimuna"; she whose "face was as a damsel's face, and yet her hair was gray"; she of whom the biographer has said, "Shelley was indeed caught in an almost invisible thread spun around him, but unconsciously, by this subtle and benignant enchantress." The subtle and benignant enchantress writes to Hogg, April 18: "Shelley is again a widower; his beauteous half went to town on Thursday."

Then Shelley writes a poem—a chant of grief over the hard fate which obliges him now to leave his paradise and take up with his wife again. It seems to intimate that the paradise is cooling toward him; that he is warned off by acclamation; that he must not even venture to tempt with one last tear his friend Cornelia's ungentle mood, for her eye is glazed and cold and dares not entreat her lover to stay:

Exhibit E

*"Pause not! the time is past! Every voice cries 'Away!'*

*Tempt not with one last tear thy friend's ungentle mood;*

*Thy lover's eye, so glazed and cold, dares not entreat thy stay:*

> *Duty and dereliction guide thee back to solitude."*

Back to the solitude of his now empty home, that is!

> *"Away! away! to thy sad and silent home;*
>
> *Pour bitter tears on its desolated hearth."*

........

But he will have rest in the grave by-and-by. Until that time comes, the charms of Bracknell will remain in his memory, along with Mrs. Boinville's voice and Cornelia Turner's smile:

> *"Thou in the grave shalt rest—yet, till the phantoms flee*
>
> *Which that house and hearth and garden made dear to thee ere while,*
>
> *Thy remembrance and repentance and deep musings are not free*
>
> *From the music of two voices and the light of one sweet smile."*

We cannot wonder that Harriet could not stand it. Any of us would have left. We would not even stay with a cat that was in this condition. Even the Boinvilles could not endure it; and so, as we have seen, they gave this one notice.

> *"Early in May, Shelley was in London. He did not yet despair*
>
> *of reconciliation with Harriet, nor had he ceased to love her."*

Shelley's poems are a good deal of trouble to his biographer. They are constantly inserted as "evidence," and they make much confusion. As soon as one of them has proved one thing, another one follows and proves quite a different thing. The poem just quoted shows that he was in love with Cornelia, but a month later he is in love with Harriet again, and there is a poem to prove it.

> *"In this piteous appeal Shelley declares that he has now no*
>
> *grief but one—the grief of having known and lost his wife's*
>
> *love."*

Exhibit F

> *"Thy look of love has power to calm*
>
> *The stormiest passion of my soul."*

But without doubt she had been reserving her looks of love a good part of the time for ten months, now—ever since he began to lavish his own on Cornelia Turner at the end of the previous July. He does really seem to have already forgotten Cornelia's merits in one brief month, for he eulogizes Harriet in a way which rules all competition out:

> *"Thou only virtuous, gentle, kind,*
>
> *Amid a world of hate."*

He complains of her hardness, and begs her to make the concession of a "slight endurance"—of his waywardness, perhaps—for the sake of "a fellow-being's lasting weal." But the main force of his appeal is in his closing stanza, and is strongly worded:

> *"O trust for once no erring guide!*
>
> *Bid the remorseless feeling flee;*
>
> *'Tis malice, 'tis revenge, 'tis pride,*
>
> *'Tis anything but thee;*
>
> *O deign a nobler pride to prove,*
>
> *And pity if thou canst not love."*

This is in May—apparently towards the end of it. Harriet and Shelley were corresponding all the time. Harriet got the poem—a copy exists in her own handwriting; she being the only gentle and kind person amid a world of hate, according to Shelley's own testimony in the poem, we are permitted to think that the daily letters would presently have melted that kind and gentle heart and brought about the reconciliation, if there had been time but there wasn't; for in a very few days—in fact, before the 8th of June—Shelley was in love with another woman.

And so—perhaps while Harriet was walking the floor nights, trying to get her poem by heart—her husband was doing a fresh one—for the other girl—Mary Wollstonecraft Godwin—with sentiments like these in it:

Exhibit G

> *To spend years thus and be rewarded,*
>
> *As thou, sweet love, requited me*
>
> *When none were near.*
>
> *... thy lips did meet*
>
> *Mine tremblingly;...*
>
> *"Gentle and good and mild thou art,*
>
> *Nor can I live if thou appear*
>
> *Aught but thyself."...*

And so on. "Before the close of June it was known and felt by Mary and Shelley that each was inexpressibly dear to the other." Yes, Shelley had found this child of sixteen to his liking, and had wooed and won her in the graveyard. But that is nothing; it was better than wooing her in her nursery, at any rate, where it might have disturbed the other children.

However, she was a child in years only. From the day that she set her masculine grip on Shelley he was to frisk no more. If she had occupied the only kind and gentle Harriet's place in March it would have been a thrilling spectacle to see her invade the Boinville rookery and read the riot act. That holiday of Shelley's would have been of short duration, and Cornelia's hair would have been as gray as her mother's when the services were over.

Hogg went to the Godwin residence in Skinner Street with Shelley on that 8th of June. They passed through Godwin's little debt-factory of a book-shop and went up-stairs hunting for the proprietor. Nobody there. Shelley strode about the room impatiently, making its crazy floor quake under him. Then a door "was partially and softly opened. A thrilling voice called 'Shelley!' A thrilling voice answered, 'Mary!' And he darted out of the room like an arrow from the bow of the far-shooting King. A very young female, fair and fair-haired, pale, indeed, and with a piercing look, wearing a frock of tartan, an unusual dress in London at that time, had called him out of the room."

This is Mary Godwin, as described by Hogg. The thrill of the voices shows that the love of Shelley and Mary was already upward of a fortnight old; therefore it had been born within the month of May—born while Harriet was still trying to get her poem by heart, we think. I must not be asked how I know so much about that thrill; it is my secret. The biographer and I have private ways of finding out things when it is necessary to find them out and the customary methods fail.

Shelley left London that day, and was gone ten days. The biographer conjectures that he spent this interval with Harriet in Bath. It would be just like him. To the end of his days he liked to be in love with two women at once. He was more in love with Miss Hitchener when he married Harriet than he was with Harriet, and told the lady so with simple and unostentatious candor. He was more in love with Cornelia than he was with Harriet in the end of 1813 and the beginning of 1814, yet he supplied both of them with love poems of an equal temperature meantime; he loved Mary and Harriet in June, and while getting ready to run off with the one, it is conjectured that he put in his odd time trying to get reconciled to the other; by-and-by, while still in love with Mary, he will make love to her half-sister by marriage, adoption, and the visitation of God, through the medium of clandestine letters, and she will answer with letters that are for no eye but his own.

When Shelley encountered Mary Godwin he was looking around for another paradise. He had tastes of his own, and there were features about the Godwin establishment that strongly recommended it. Godwin was an advanced thinker and an able writer. One of his romances is still read, but his philosophical works, once so esteemed, are out of vogue now; their authority was already declining when Shelley made his acquaintance —that is, it was declining with the public, but not with Shelley. They had been his moral and political Bible, and they were that yet. Shelley the infidel would himself have claimed to be less a work of God than a work of Godwin. Godwin's philosophies had formed his mind and interwoven themselves into it and become a part of its texture; he regarded himself as Godwin's spiritual son. Godwin was not without self-appreciation; indeed, it may be conjectured that from his point of view the last syllable of his name was surplusage. He lived serene in his lofty world of philosophy, far above the mean interests that absorbed smaller men, and only came down to the ground at intervals to pass the hat for alms to pay his debts with, and insult the man that relieved him. Several of his principles were out of the ordinary. For example, he was opposed to marriage. He was not aware that his preachings from this text were but theory and wind; he supposed he was in earnest in imploring people to live together without marrying, until Shelley furnished him a working model of his scheme and a practical example to analyze, by applying the principle in his own family; the matter took a different and surprising aspect then. The late Matthew Arnold said that the main defect in Shelley's make-up was that he was destitute of the sense of humor. This episode must have escaped Mr. Arnold's attention.

But we have said enough about the head of the new paradise. Mrs. Godwin is described as being in several ways a terror; and even when her soul was in repose she wore green spectacles. But I suspect that her main unattractiveness was born of the fact that she wrote the letters that are out in the appendix-basket in the back yard—letters which are an outrage and wholly untrustworthy, for they say some kind things about poor Harriet and tell some disagreeable truths about her husband; and these things make the fabulist grit his teeth a good deal.

Next we have Fanny Godwin—a Godwin by courtesy only; she was Mrs. Godwin's natural daughter by a former friend. She was a sweet and winning girl, but she presently wearied of the Godwin paradise, and poisoned herself.

Last in the list is Jane (or Claire, as she preferred to call herself) Clairmont, daughter of Mrs. Godwin by a former marriage. She was very young and pretty and accommodating, and always ready to do what she could to make things pleasant. After Shelley ran off with her part-sister Mary, she became the guest of the pair, and contributed a natural child to their nursery—Allegra. Lord Byron was the father.

We have named the several members and advantages of the new paradise in Skinner Street, with its crazy book-shop underneath. Shelley was all right now, this was a better place than the other; more variety anyway, and more different kinds of fragrance. One could turn out poetry here without any trouble at all.

The way the new love-match came about was this:

Shelley told Mary all his aggravations and sorrows and griefs, and about the wet-nurse and the bonnetshop and the surgeon and the carriage, and the sister-in-law that blocked the London game, and about Cornelia and her mamma, and how they had turned him out of the house after making so much of him; and how he had deserted Harriet and then Harriet had deserted him, and how the reconciliation was working along and Harriet getting her poem by heart; and still he was not happy, and Mary pitied him, for she had had trouble herself. But I am not satisfied with this. It reads too much like statistics. It lacks smoothness and grace, and is too earthy and business-like. It has the sordid look of a trades-union procession out on strike. That is not the right form for it. The book does it better; we will fall back on the book and have a cake-walk:

> "It was easy to divine that some restless grief possessed him; Mary herself was not unlearned in the lore of pain. His generous zeal in her father's behalf, his spiritual sonship to Godwin, his reverence for her mother's memory, were guarantees with Mary of his excellence.—[What she was after was guarantees of his excellence. That he stood ready to desert his wife and child was one of them, apparently.]—The new friends could not lack subjects of discourse, and underneath their words about Mary's mother, and 'Political Justice,' and 'Rights of Woman,' were two young hearts, each feeling towards

> *the other, each perhaps unaware, trembling in the direction of the other. The desire to assuage the suffering of one whose happiness has grown precious to us may become a hunger of the spirit as keen as any other, and this hunger now possessed Mary's heart; when her eyes rested unseen on Shelley, it was with a look full of the ardor of a 'soothing pity.'"*

Yes, that is better and has more composure. That is just the way it happened. He told her about the wet-nurse, she told him about political justice; he told her about the deadly sister-in-law, she told him about her mother; he told her about the bonnet-shop, she murmured back about the rights of woman; then he assuaged her, then she assuaged him; then he assuaged her some more, next she assuaged him some more; then they both assuaged one another simultaneously; and so they went on by the hour assuaging and assuaging and assuaging, until at last what was the result? They were in love. It will happen so every time.

> *"He had married a woman who, as he now persuaded himself, had never truly loved him, who loved only his fortune and his rank, and who proved her selfishness by deserting him in his misery."*

I think that that is not quite fair to Harriet. We have no certainty that she knew Cornelia had turned him out of the house. He went back to Cornelia, and Harriet may have supposed that he was as happy with her as ever. Still, it was judicious to begin to lay on the whitewash, for Shelley is going to need many a coat of it now, and the sooner the reader becomes used to the intrusion of the brush the sooner he will get reconciled to it and stop fretting about it.

After Shelley's (conjectured) visit to Harriet at Bath—8th of June to 18th—"it seems to have been arranged that Shelley should henceforth join the Skinner Street household each day at dinner."

Nothing could be handier than this; things will swim along now.

> *"Although now Shelley was coming to believe that his wedded union with Harriet was a thing of the past, he had not ceased to regard her with affectionate consideration; he wrote to her frequently, and kept her informed of his whereabouts."*

We must not get impatient over these curious inharmoniousnesses and irreconcilabilities in Shelley's character. You can see by the biographer's attitude towards them that there is nothing objectionable about them. Shelley was doing his best to make two adoring young creatures happy: he was regarding the one with affectionate consideration by mail, and he was assuaging the other one at home.

> *"Unhappy Harriet, residing at Bath, had perhaps never desired that the breach between herself and her husband should be irreparable and complete."*

I find no fault with that sentence except that the "perhaps" is not strictly warranted. It should have been left out. In support—or shall we say extenuation?—of this opinion I submit that there is not sufficient evidence to warrant the uncertainty which it implies. The only "evidence" offered that Harriet was hard and proud and standing out against a reconciliation is a poem—the poem in which Shelley beseeches her to "bid the remorseless feeling flee" and "pity" if she "cannot love." We have just that as "evidence," and out of its meagre materials the biographer builds a cobhouse of conjectures as big as the Coliseum; conjectures which convince him, the prosecuting attorney, but ought to fall far short of convincing any fair-minded jury.

Shelley's love-poems may be very good evidence, but we know well that they are "good for this day and train only." We are able to believe that they spoke the truth for that one day, but we know by experience that they could not be depended on to speak it the next. The very supplication for a rewarming of Harriet's chilled love was followed so suddenly by the poet's plunge into an adoring passion for Mary Godwin that if it had been a check it would have lost its value before a lazy person could have gotten to the bank with it.

Hardness, stubbornness, pride, vindictiveness—these may sometimes reside in a young wife and mother of nineteen, but they are not charged against Harriet Shelley outside of that poem, and one has no right to insert them into her character on such shadowy "evidence" as that. Peacock knew Harriet well, and she has a flexible and persuadable look, as painted by him:

> "Her manners were good, and her whole aspect and demeanor such manifest emanations of pure and truthful nature that to be once in her company was to know her thoroughly. She was fond of her husband, and accommodated herself in every way to his tastes. If they mixed in society, she adorned it; if they lived in retirement, she was satisfied; if they travelled, she enjoyed the change of scene."

"Perhaps" she had never desired that the breach should be irreparable and complete. The truth is, we do not even know that there was any breach at all at this time. We know that the husband and wife went before the altar and took a new oath on the 24th of March to love and cherish each other until death—and this may be regarded as a sort of reconciliation itself, and a wiping out of the old grudges. Then Harriet went away, and the sister-in-law removed herself from her society. That was in April. Shelley wrote his "appeal" in May, but the corresponding went right along afterwards. We have a right to doubt that the subject of it was a "reconciliation," or that Harriet had any suspicion that she needed to be reconciled and that her husband was trying to persuade her to it—as the biographer has sought to make us believe, with his Coliseum of conjectures built out of a waste-basket of poetry. For we have "evidence" now—not poetry and conjecture. When Shelley had been dining daily in the Skinner Street paradise fifteen days and continuing the love-match which was already a fortnight old twenty-five days earlier, he forgot to write Harriet; forgot it the next day and the next. During four days Harriet got no letter from him. Then her fright and anxiety rose to expression-heat, and she wrote a letter to Shelley's publisher which seems to reveal to us that Shelley's letters to her had been the customary affectionate letters of husband to wife, and had carried no appeals for reconciliation and had not needed to:

"BATH *(postmark July 7, 1814).*

*"MY DEAR SIR,—You will greatly oblige me by giving the enclosed to Mr. Shelley. I would not trouble you, but it is now four days since I have heard from him, which to me is an age. Will you write by return of post and tell me what has become of him? as I always fancy something dreadful has happened if I do not hear from him. If you tell me that he is well I shall not come to London, but if I do not hear from you or him I shall certainly come, as I cannot endure this dreadful state of suspense. You are his friend and you can feel for me.*

*"I remain yours truly,*

*"H. S."*

Even without Peacock's testimony that "her whole aspect and demeanor were manifest emanations of a pure and truthful nature," we should hold this to be a truthful letter, a sincere letter, a loving letter; it bears those marks; I think it is also the letter of a person accustomed to receiving letters from her husband frequently, and that they have been of a welcome and satisfactory sort, too, this long time back—ever since the solemn remarriage and reconciliation at the altar most likely.

The biographer follows Harriet's letter with a conjecture. He conjectures that she "would now gladly have retraced her steps." Which means that it is proven that she had steps to retrace—proven by the poem. Well, if the poem is better evidence than the letter, we must let it stand at that.

Then the biographer attacks Harriet Shelley's honor—by authority of random and unverified gossip scavengered from a group of people whose very names make a person shudder: Mary Godwin, mistress to Shelley; her part-sister, discarded mistress of Lord Byron; Godwin, the philosophical tramp, who gathers his share of it from a shadow—that is to say, from a person whom he shirks out of naming. Yet the biographer dignifies this sorry rubbish with the name of "evidence."

Nothing remotely resembling a distinct charge from a named person professing to know is offered among this precious "evidence."

1. "Shelley believed" so and so.

2. Byron's discarded mistress says that Shelley told Mary Godwin so and so, and Mary told her.

3. "Shelley said" so and so—and later "admitted over and over again that he had been in error."

4. The unspeakable Godwin "wrote to Mr. Baxter" that he knew so and so "from unquestionable authority"—name not furnished.

How any man in his right mind could bring himself to defile the grave of a shamefully abused and defenseless girl with these baseless fabrications, this manufactured filth, is inconceivable. How any man, in his right mind or out of it, could sit down and coldly try to persuade anybody to believe it, or listen patiently to it, or, indeed, do anything but scoff at it and deride it, is astonishing.

The charge insinuated by these odious slanders is one of the most difficult of all offenses to prove; it is also one which no man has a right to mention even in a whisper about any woman, living or dead, unless he knows it to be true, and not even then unless he can also prove it to be true. There is no justification for the abomination of putting this stuff in the book.

Against Harriet Shelley's good name there is not one scrap of tarnishing evidence, and not even a scrap of evil gossip, that comes from a source that entitles it to a hearing.

On the credit side of the account we have strong opinions from the people who knew her best. Peacock says:

> "I feel it due to the memory of Harriet to state my most decided conviction that her conduct as a wife was as pure, as true, as absolutely faultless, as that of any who for such conduct are held most in honor."

Thornton Hunt, who had picked and published slight flaws in Harriet's character, says, as regards this alleged large one:

> "There is not a trace of evidence or a whisper of scandal against her before her voluntary departure from Shelley."

Trelawney says:

> "I was assured by the evidence of the few friends who knew both Shelley and his wife—Hookham, Hogg, Peacock, and one of the Godwins—that Harriet was perfectly innocent of all offense."

What excuse was there for raking up a parcel of foul rumors from malicious and discredited sources and flinging them at this dead girl's head? Her very defenselessness should have been her protection. The fact that all letters to her or about her, with almost every scrap of her own writing, had been diligently mislaid, leaving her case destitute of a voice, while every pen-stroke which could help her husband's side had been as diligently preserved, should have excused her from being brought to trial. Her witnesses have all disappeared, yet we see her summoned in her grave-clothes to plead for the life of her character, without the help of an advocate, before a disqualified judge and a packed jury.

Harriet Shelley wrote her distressed letter on the 7th of July. On the 28th her husband ran away with Mary Godwin and her part-sister Claire to the Continent. He deserted his wife when her confinement was approaching. She bore him a child at the end of November, his mistress bore him another one something over two months later. The truants were back in London before either of these events occurred.

On one occasion, presently, Shelley was so pressed for money to support his mistress with that he went to his wife and got some money of his that was in her hands—twenty pounds. Yet the mistress was not moved to gratitude; for later, when the wife was troubled to meet her engagements, the mistress makes this entry in her diary:

> "*Harriet sends her creditors here; nasty woman. Now we shall*
>
> *have to change our lodgings.*"

The deserted wife bore the bitterness and obloquy of her situation two years and a quarter; then she gave up, and drowned herself. A month afterwards the body was found in the water. Three weeks later Shelley married his mistress.

I must here be allowed to italicize a remark of the biographer's concerning Harriet Shelley:

> "*That no act of Shelley's during the two years which*
>
> *immediately preceded her death tended to cause the rash act*
>
> *which brought her life to its close seems certain.*"

Yet her husband had deserted her and her children, and was living with a concubine all that time! Why should a person attempt to write biography when the simplest facts have no meaning to him? This book is littered with as crass stupidities as that one—deductions by the page which bear no discoverable kinship to their premises.

The biographer throws off that extraordinary remark without any perceptible disturbance to his serenity; for he follows it with a sentimental justification of Shelley's conduct which has not a pang of conscience in it, but is silky and smooth and undulating and pious—a cake-walk with all the colored brethren at their best. There may be people who can read that page and keep their temper, but it is doubtful. Shelley's life has the one indelible blot upon it, but is otherwise worshipfully noble and beautiful. It even stands out indestructibly gracious and lovely from the ruck of these disastrous pages, in spite of the fact that they expose and establish his responsibility for his forsaken wife's pitiful fate—a responsibility which he himself tacitly admits in a letter to Eliza Westbrook, wherein he refers to his taking up with Mary Godwin as an act which Eliza "might excusably regard as the cause of her sister's ruin."

# About Author

Samuel Langhorne Clemens (November 30, 1835 – April 21, 1910), known by his pen name Mark Twain, was an American writer, humorist, entrepreneur, publisher, and lecturer. He was lauded as the "greatest humorist this country has produced", and William Faulkner called him "the father of American literature". His novels include The Adventures of Tom Sawyer (1876) and its sequel, the Adventures of Huckleberry Finn (1884), the latter often called "The Great American Novel".

Twain was raised in Hannibal, Missouri, which later provided the setting for Tom Sawyer and Huckleberry Finn. He served an apprenticeship with a printer and then worked as a typesetter, contributing articles to the newspaper of his older brother Orion Clemens. He later became a riverboat pilot on the Mississippi River before heading west to join Orion in Nevada. He referred humorously to his lack of success at mining, turning to journalism for the Virginia City Territorial Enterprise. His humorous story, "The Celebrated Jumping Frog of Calaveras County", was published in 1865, based on a story that he heard at Angels Hotel in Angels Camp, California, where he had spent some time as a miner. The short story brought international attention and was even translated into French. His wit and satire, in prose and in speech, earned praise from critics and peers, and he was a friend to presidents, artists, industrialists, and European royalty.

Twain earned a great deal of money from his writings and lectures, but he invested in ventures that lost most of it—such as the Paige Compositor, a mechanical typesetter that failed because of its complexity and imprecision. He filed for bankruptcy in the wake of these financial setbacks, but he eventually overcame his financial troubles with the help of Henry Huttleston Rogers. He eventually paid all his creditors in full, even though his bankruptcy relieved him of having to do so.

Twain was born shortly after an appearance of Halley's Comet, and he predicted that he would "go out with it" as well; he died the day after the comet returned.

## Biography

### Early life

Samuel Langhorne Clemens was born on November 30, 1835, in Florida, Missouri, the sixth of seven children born to Jane (née Lampton; 1803–1890), a native of Kentucky, and John Marshall Clemens (1798–1847), a native of Virginia. His parents met when his father moved to Missouri, and they were married in 1823. Twain was of Cornish, English, and Scots-Irish descent. Only three of his siblings survived childhood: Orion (1825–1897), Henry (1838–1858), and Pamela (1827–1904). His sister Margaret (1830–1839) died when Twain was three, and his brother Benjamin (1832–1842) died three years later. His brother Pleasant Hannibal (1828) died at three weeks of age.

When he was four, Twain's family moved to Hannibal, Missouri, a port town on the Mississippi River that inspired the fictional town of St. Petersburg in The Adventures of Tom Sawyer and the Adventures of Huckleberry Finn. Slavery was legal in Missouri at the time, and it became a theme in these writings. His father was an attorney and judge, who died of pneumonia in 1847, when Twain was 11. The next year, Twain left school after the fifth grade to become a printer's apprentice. In 1851, he began working as a typesetter, contributing articles and humorous sketches to the Hannibal Journal, a newspaper that Orion owned. When he was 18, he left Hannibal and worked as a printer in New York City, Philadelphia, St. Louis, and Cincinnati, joining the newly formed International Typographical Union, the printers trade union. He educated himself in public libraries in the evenings, finding wider information than at a conventional school.

Twain describes his boyhood in Life on the Mississippi, stating that "there was but one permanent ambition" among his comrades: to be a steamboatman.

Pilot was the grandest position of all. The pilot, even in those days of trivial wages, had a princely salary – from a hundred and fifty to two hundred and fifty dollars a month, and no board to pay.

As Twain describes it, the pilot's prestige exceeded that of the captain. The pilot had to:

> ...get up a warm personal acquaintanceship with every old snag and one-limbed cottonwood and every obscure wood pile that ornaments the banks of this river for twelve hundred miles; and more than that, must... actually know where these things are in the dark

Steamboat pilot Horace E. Bixby took Twain on as a cub pilot to teach him the river between New Orleans and St. Louis for $500 (equivalent to $14,000 in 2018), payable out of Twain's first wages after graduating. Twain studied the Mississippi, learning its landmarks, how to navigate its currents effectively, and how to read the river and its constantly shifting channels, reefs, submerged snags, and rocks that would "tear the life out of the strongest vessel that ever floated". It was more than two years before he received his pilot's license. Piloting also gave him his pen name from "mark twain", the leadsman's cry for a measured river depth of two fathoms (12 feet), which was safe water for a steamboat.

As a young pilot, Clemens served on the steamer A. B. Chambers with Grant Marsh, who became famous for his exploits as a steamboat captain on the Missouri River. The two liked each other, and admired one another, and maintained a correspondence for many years after Clemens left the river.

While training, Samuel convinced his younger brother Henry to work with him, and even arranged a post of mud clerk for him on the steamboat Pennsylvania. On June 13, 1858, the steamboat's boiler exploded; Henry succumbed to his wounds on June 21. Twain claimed to have foreseen this death in a dream a month earlier, which inspired his interest in parapsychology; he was an early member of the Society for Psychical Research. Twain was guilt-stricken and held himself responsible for the rest of his life. He continued to work on the river and was a river pilot until the Civil War broke out in 1861, when traffic was curtailed along the Mississippi River. At the start of hostilities, he enlisted briefly in a local Confederate unit. He later wrote the sketch "The Private History of a Campaign That Failed", describing how he and his friends had been Confederate volunteers for two weeks before disbanding.

He then left for Nevada to work for his brother Orion, who was Secretary of the Nevada Territory. Twain describes the episode in his book Roughing It.

**Travels**

Orion became secretary to Nevada Territory governor James W. Nye in 1861, and Twain joined him when he moved west. The brothers traveled more than two weeks on a stagecoach across the Great Plains and the Rocky Mountains, visiting the Mormon community in Salt Lake City.

Twain's journey ended in the silver-mining town of Virginia City, Nevada, where he became a miner on the Comstock Lode. He failed as a miner and went to work at the Virginia City newspaper Territorial Enterprise, working under a friend, the writer Dan DeQuille. He first used his pen name here on February 3, 1863, when he wrote a humorous travel account entitled "Letter From Carson – re: Joe Goodman; party at Gov. Johnson's; music" and signed it "Mark Twain".

His experiences in the American West inspired Roughing It, written during 1870–71 and published in 1872. His experiences in Angels Camp (in Calaveras County, California) provided material for "The Celebrated Jumping Frog of Calaveras County" (1865).

Twain moved to San Francisco in 1864, still as a journalist, and met writers such as Bret Harte and Artemus Ward. He may have been romantically involved with the poet Ina Coolbrith.

His first success as a writer came when his humorous tall tale "The Celebrated Jumping Frog of Calaveras County" was published on November 18, 1865, in the New York weekly The Saturday Press, bringing him national attention. A year later, he traveled to the Sandwich Islands (present-day Hawaii) as a reporter for the Sacramento Union. His letters to the Union were popular and became the basis for his first lectures.

In 1867, a local newspaper funded his trip to the Mediterranean aboard the Quaker City, including a tour of Europe and the Middle East. He wrote a collection of travel letters which were later compiled as The Innocents Abroad (1869). It was on this trip that he met fellow passenger Charles Langdon, who showed him a picture of his sister Olivia. Twain later claimed to have fallen in love at first sight.

Upon returning to the United States, Twain was offered honorary membership in Yale University's secret society Scroll and Key in 1868. Its devotion to "fellowship, moral and literary self-improvement, and charity" suited him well.

**Marriage and children**

Twain and Olivia Langdon corresponded throughout 1868. She rejected his first marriage proposal, but they were married in Elmira, New York in February 1870, where he courted her and managed to overcome her father's initial reluctance. She came from a "wealthy but liberal family"; through her, he met abolitionists, "socialists, principled atheists and activists for women's rights and social equality", including Harriet Beecher Stowe (his next-door neighbor in Hartford, Connecticut), Frederick Douglass, and writer and utopian socialist William Dean Howells, who became a long-time friend. The couple lived in Buffalo, New York, from 1869 to 1871. He owned a stake in the Buffalo Express newspaper and worked as an editor and writer. While they were living in Buffalo, their son Langdon died of diphtheria at the age of 19 months. They had three daughters: Susy (1872–1896), Clara (1874–1962), and Jean (1880–1909).

Twain moved his family to Hartford, Connecticut, where he arranged the building of a home starting in 1873. In the 1870s and 1880s, the family summered at Quarry Farm in Elmira, the home of Olivia's sister, Susan Crane. In 1874, Susan had a study built apart from the main house so that Twain would have a quiet place in which to write. Also, he smoked cigars constantly, and Susan did not want him to do so in her house.

Twain wrote many of his classic novels during his 17 years in Hartford (1874–1891) and over 20 summers at Quarry Farm. They include The Adventures of Tom Sawyer (1876), The Prince and the Pauper (1881), Life on the Mississippi (1883), Adventures of Huckleberry Finn (1884), and A

Connecticut Yankee in King Arthur's Court (1889).

The couple's marriage lasted 34 years until Olivia's death in 1904. All of the Clemens family are buried in Elmira's Woodlawn Cemetery.

**Love of science and technology**

Twain was fascinated with science and scientific inquiry. He developed a close and lasting friendship with Nikola Tesla, and the two spent much time together in Tesla's laboratory.

Twain patented three inventions, including an "Improvement in Adjustable and Detachable Straps for Garments" (to replace suspenders) and a history trivia game. Most commercially successful was a self-pasting scrapbook; a dried adhesive on the pages needed only to be moistened before use. Over 25,000 were sold.

Twain was an early proponent of fingerprinting as a forensic technique, featuring it in a tall tale in Life on the Mississippi (1883) and as a central plot element in the novel Pudd'nhead Wilson (1894).

Twain's novel A Connecticut Yankee in King Arthur's Court (1889) features a time traveler from the contemporary U.S., using his knowledge of science to introduce modern technology to Arthurian England. This type of historical manipulation became a trope of speculative fiction as alternate histories.

In 1909, Thomas Edison visited Twain at his home in Redding, Connecticut and filmed him. Part of the footage was used in The Prince and the Pauper (1909), a two-reel short film. It is the only known existing film footage of Twain.

**Financial troubles**

Twain made a substantial amount of money through his writing, but he lost a great deal through investments. He invested mostly in new inventions and technology, particularly the Paige typesetting machine. It was a beautifully engineered mechanical marvel that amazed viewers when it worked, but it was prone to breakdowns. Twain spent $300,000 (equal to $9,000,000 in inflation-adjusted terms) on it between 1880 and 1894, but before it could be perfected it was rendered obsolete by the Linotype. He lost the bulk of his book profits, as well as a substantial portion of his wife's inheritance.

Twain also lost money through his publishing house, Charles L. Webster and Company, which enjoyed initial success selling the memoirs of Ulysses S. Grant but failed soon afterward, losing money on a biography of Pope Leo XIII. Fewer than 200 copies were sold.

Twain and his family closed down their expensive Hartford home in response to the dwindling income and moved to Europe in June 1891. William M. Laffan of The New York Sun and the McClure Newspaper Syndicate offered him the publication of a series of six European letters. Twain, Olivia, and their daughter Susy were all faced with health problems, and they believed that it would be of benefit to visit European baths. The family stayed mainly in France, Germany, and Italy until May 1895, with longer spells at Berlin (winter 1891/92), Florence (fall and winter 1892/93), and Paris (winters and springs 1893/94 and 1894/95). During that period, Twain returned four times to New York due to his enduring business troubles. He took "a cheap room" in September 1893 at $1.50 per day (equivalent to $42 in 2018) at The Players Club, which he had to keep until March 1894; meanwhile, he became "the Belle of New York," in the words of biographer Albert Bigelow Paine.

Twain's writings and lectures enabled him to recover financially, combined with the help of his friend, Henry Huttleston Rogers. He began a friendship with the financier in 1893, a principal of Standard Oil, that lasted the remainder of his life. Rogers first made him file for bankruptcy in April 1894, then had him transfer the copyrights on his written works to his wife to prevent creditors from gaining possession of them. Finally, Rogers took absolute charge of Twain's money until all his creditors were paid.

Twain accepted an offer from Robert Sparrow Smythe and embarked on a year-long, around the world lecture tour in July 1895 to pay off his creditors in full, although he was no longer under any legal obligation to do so. It was a long, arduous journey and he was sick much of the time, mostly from a cold and a carbuncle. The first part of the itinerary took him across northern America to British Columbia, Canada, until the second half of August. For the second part, he sailed across the Pacific Ocean. His scheduled lecture in Honolulu, Hawaii had to be canceled due to a cholera epidemic. Twain went on to Fiji, Australia, New Zealand, Sri Lanka, India, Mauritius, and South Africa. His three months in India became the centerpiece of his 712-page book Following the Equator. In the second half of July 1896, he sailed back to England, completing his circumnavigation of the world begun 14 months before.

Twain and his family spent four more years in Europe, mainly in England and Austria (October 1897 to May 1899), with longer spells in London and Vienna. Clara had wished to study the piano under Theodor Leschetizky in Vienna. However, Jean's health did not benefit from consulting with specialists in Vienna, the "City of Doctors". The family moved to London in spring 1899, following a lead by Poultney Bigelow who had a good experience being treated by Dr. Jonas Henrik Kellgren, a Swedish osteopathic practitioner in Belgravia. They were persuaded to spend the summer at Kellgren's sanatorium by the lake in the Swedish village of Sanna. Coming back in fall, they continued the treatment in London, until Twain was convinced by lengthy inquiries in America that similar osteopathic expertise was available there.

In mid-1900, he was the guest of newspaper proprietor Hugh Gilzean-Reid at Dollis Hill House, located on the north side of London. Twain wrote that he had "never seen any place that was so satisfactorily situated, with its noble trees and stretch of country, and everything that went to make life delightful, and all within a biscuit's throw of the metropolis of the world." He then returned to America in October 1900, having earned enough to pay off his debts. In winter 1900/01, he became his country's most prominent opponent of imperialism, raising the issue in his speeches, interviews, and writings. In January 1901, he began serving as vice-president of the Anti-Imperialist League of New York.

**Speaking engagements**

Twain was in great demand as a featured speaker, performing solo humorous talks similar to modern stand-up comedy. He gave paid talks to many men's clubs, including the Authors' Club, Beefsteak Club, Vagabonds, White Friars, and Monday Evening Club of Hartford.

In the late 1890s, he spoke to the Savage Club in London and was elected an honorary member. He was told that only three men had been so honored, including the Prince of Wales, and he replied: "Well, it must make the Prince feel mighty fine." He visited Melbourne and Sydney in 1895 as part of a world lecture tour. In 1897, he spoke to the Concordia Press Club in Vienna as a special guest, following the diplomat Charlemagne Tower, Jr. He delivered the speech "Die Schrecken der Deutschen Sprache" ("The Horrors of the German Language")—in German—to the great amusement of the audience. In 1901, he was invited to speak at Princeton University's Cliosophic Literary Society, where he was made an honorary member.

**Canadian visits**

In 1881, Twain was honored at a banquet in Montreal, Canada where he made reference to securing a copyright. In 1883, he paid a brief visit to Ottawa, and he visited Toronto twice in 1884 and 1885 on a reading tour with George Washington Cable, known as the "Twins of Genius" tour.

The reason for the Toronto visits was to secure Canadian and British copyrights for his upcoming book Adventures of Huckleberry Finn, to which he had alluded in his Montreal visit. The reason for the Ottawa visit had been to secure Canadian and British copyrights for Life on the Mississippi. Publishers in Toronto had printed unauthorized editions of his books at the time, before an international copyright agreement was established in 1891. These were sold in the United States as well as in Canada, depriving him of royalties. He estimated that Belford Brothers' edition of The Adventures of Tom Sawyer alone had cost him ten thousand dollars (equivalent to $280,000 in 2018). He had unsuccessfully attempted to secure the rights for The Prince and the Pauper in 1881, in conjunction with his Montreal trip. Eventually, he received legal advice to register a copyright in Canada (for both Canada and Britain) prior to publishing in the United States, which would restrain the Canadian publishers from printing a version when the American edition was published. There was a requirement that a copyright be registered to a Canadian resident; he addressed this by his short visits to the country.

## Later life and death

... the report is greatly exaggerated.

—Twain's reaction to a report of his death

Twain lived in his later years at 14 West 10th Street in Manhattan. He passed through a period of deep depression which began in 1896 when his daughter Susy died of meningitis. Olivia's death in 1904 and Jean's on December 24, 1909, deepened his gloom. On May 20, 1909, his close friend Henry Rogers died suddenly. In 1906, Twain began his autobiography in the North American Review. In April, he heard that his friend Ina Coolbrith had lost nearly all that she owned in the 1906 San Francisco earthquake, and he volunteered a few autographed portrait photographs to be sold for her benefit. To further aid Coolbrith, George Wharton James visited Twain in New York and arranged for a new portrait session. He was resistant initially, but he eventually admitted that four of the resulting images were the finest ones ever taken of him.

Twain formed a club in 1906 for girls whom he viewed as surrogate granddaughters called the Angel Fish and Aquarium Club. The dozen or so members ranged in age from 10 to 16. He exchanged letters with his "Angel Fish" girls and invited them to concerts and the theatre and to play games. Twain wrote in 1908 that the club was his "life's chief delight". In 1907, he met Dorothy Quick (aged 11) on a transatlantic crossing, beginning "a friendship that was to last until the very day of his death".

Oxford University awarded Twain an honorary doctorate in letters in 1907.

Twain was born two weeks after Halley's Comet's closest approach in 1835; he said in 1909:

I came in with Halley's Comet in 1835. It is coming again next year, and I expect to go out with it. It will be the greatest disappointment of my life if

I don't go out with Halley's Comet. The Almighty has said, no doubt: "Now here are these two unaccountable freaks; they came in together, they must go out together".

Twain's prediction was accurate; he died of a heart attack on April 21, 1910, in Redding, Connecticut, one day after the comet's closest approach to Earth.

Upon hearing of Twain's death, President William Howard Taft said:

Mark Twain gave pleasure – real intellectual enjoyment – to millions, and his works will continue to give such pleasure to millions yet to come … His humor was American, but he was nearly as much appreciated by Englishmen and people of other countries as by his own countrymen. He has made an enduring part of American literature.

Twain's funeral was at the Brick Presbyterian Church on Fifth Avenue, New York. He is buried in his wife's family plot at Woodlawn Cemetery in Elmira, New York. The Langdon family plot is marked by a 12-foot monument (two fathoms, or "mark twain") placed there by his surviving daughter Clara. There is also a smaller headstone. He expressed a preference for cremation (for example, in Life on the Mississippi), but he acknowledged that his surviving family would have the last word.

Officials in Connecticut and New York estimated the value of Twain's estate at $471,000 ($13,000,000 today).

**Writing**

**Overview**

Twain began his career writing light, humorous verse, but he became a chronicler of the vanities, hypocrisies, and murderous acts of mankind. At mid-career, he combined rich humor, sturdy narrative, and social criticism in Huckleberry Finn. He was a master of rendering colloquial speech and helped to create and popularize a distinctive American literature built on American themes and language.

Many of his works have been suppressed at times for various reasons. The

Adventures of Huckleberry Finn has been repeatedly restricted in American high schools, not least for its frequent use of the word "nigger", which was in common usage in the pre-Civil War period in which the novel was set.

A complete bibliography of Twain's works is nearly impossible to compile because of the vast number of pieces he wrote (often in obscure newspapers) and his use of several different pen names. Additionally, a large portion of his speeches and lectures have been lost or were not recorded; thus, the compilation of Twain's works is an ongoing process. Researchers rediscovered published material as recently as 1995 and 2015.

### Early journalism and travelogues

Twain was writing for the Virginia City newspaper the Territorial Enterprise in 1863 when he met lawyer Tom Fitch, editor of the competing newspaper Virginia Daily Union and known as the "silver-tongued orator of the Pacific". He credited Fitch with giving him his "first really profitable lesson" in writing. "When I first began to lecture, and in my earlier writings," Twain later commented, "my sole idea was to make comic capital out of everything I saw and heard." In 1866, he presented his lecture on the Sandwich Islands to a crowd in Washoe City, Nevada. Afterwards, Fitch told him:

Clemens, your lecture was magnificent. It was eloquent, moving, sincere. Never in my entire life have I listened to such a magnificent piece of descriptive narration. But you committed one unpardonable sin – the unpardonable sin. It is a sin you must never commit again. You closed a most eloquent description, by which you had keyed your audience up to a pitch of the intensest interest, with a piece of atrocious anti-climax which nullified all the really fine effect you had produced.

It was in these days that Twain became a writer of the Sagebrush School; he was known later as its most famous member. His first important work was "The Celebrated Jumping Frog of Calaveras County," published in the New York Saturday Press on November 18, 1865. After a burst of popularity, the Sacramento Union commissioned him to write letters about his travel experiences. The first journey that he took for this job was to ride the steamer Ajax on its maiden voyage to the Sandwich Islands (Hawaii).

All the while, he was writing letters to the newspaper that were meant for publishing, chronicling his experiences with humor. These letters proved to be the genesis to his work with the San Francisco Alta California newspaper, which designated him a traveling correspondent for a trip from San Francisco to New York City via the Panama isthmus.

On June 8, 1867, he set sail on the pleasure cruiser Quaker City for five months, and this trip resulted in The Innocents Abroad or The New Pilgrims' Progress. In 1872, he published his second piece of travel literature, Roughing It, as an account of his journey from Missouri to Nevada, his subsequent life in the American West, and his visit to Hawaii. The book lampoons American and Western society in the same way that Innocents critiqued the various countries of Europe and the Middle East. His next work was The Gilded Age: A Tale of Today, his first attempt at writing a novel. The book, written with his neighbor Charles Dudley Warner, is also his only collaboration.

Twain's next work drew on his experiences on the Mississippi River. Old Times on the Mississippi was a series of sketches published in the Atlantic Monthly in 1875 featuring his disillusionment with Romanticism. Old Times eventually became the starting point for Life on the Mississippi.

**Tom Sawyer and Huckleberry Finn**

Twain's next major publication was The Adventures of Tom Sawyer, which draws on his youth in Hannibal. Tom Sawyer was modeled on Twain as a child, with traces of schoolmates John Briggs and Will Bowen. The book also introduces Huckleberry Finn in a supporting role, based on Twain's boyhood friend Tom Blankenship.

The Prince and the Pauper was not as well received, despite a storyline that is common in film and literature today. The book tells the story of two boys born on the same day who are physically identical, acting as a social commentary as the prince and pauper switch places. Twain had started Adventures of Huckleberry Finn (which he consistently had problems completing) and had completed his travel book A Tramp Abroad, which describes his travels through central and southern Europe.

Twain's next major published work was the Adventures of Huckleberry Finn, which confirmed him as a noteworthy American writer. Some have called it the first Great American Novel, and the book has become required reading in many schools throughout the United States. Huckleberry Finn was an offshoot from Tom Sawyer and had a more serious tone than its predecessor. Four hundred manuscript pages were written in mid-1876, right after the publication of Tom Sawyer. The last fifth of Huckleberry Finn is subject to much controversy. Some say that Twain experienced a "failure of nerve," as critic Leo Marx puts it. Ernest Hemingway once said of Huckleberry Finn:

If you read it, you must stop where the Nigger Jim is stolen from the boys. That is the real end. The rest is just cheating.

Hemingway also wrote in the same essay:

All modern American literature comes from one book by Mark Twain called Huckleberry Finn.

Near the completion of Huckleberry Finn, Twain wrote Life on the Mississippi, which is said to have heavily influenced the novel. The travel work recounts Twain's memories and new experiences after a 22-year absence from the Mississippi River. In it, he also explains that "Mark Twain" was the call made when the boat was in safe water, indicating a depth of two fathoms (12 feet or 3.7 metres).

**Later writing**

Twain produced President Ulysses S. Grant's Memoirs through his fledgling publishing house, Charles L. Webster & Company, which he co-owned with Charles L. Webster, his nephew by marriage.

At this time he also wrote "The Private History of a Campaign That Failed" for The Century Magazine. This piece detailed his two-week stint in a Confederate militia during the Civil War. He next focused on A Connecticut Yankee in King Arthur's Court, written with the same historical fiction style as The Prince and the Pauper. A Connecticut Yankee showed the absurdities of political and social norms by setting them in the court of King Arthur. The book was started in December 1885, then shelved a few months later until the summer of 1887, and eventually finished in the spring of 1889.

His next large-scale work was Pudd'nhead Wilson, which he wrote rapidly, as he was desperately trying to stave off bankruptcy. From November 12 to December 14, 1893, Twain wrote 60,000 words for the novel. Critics[who?] have pointed to this rushed completion as the cause of the novel's rough organization and constant disruption of the plot. This novel also contains the tale of two boys born on the same day who switch positions in life, like The Prince and the Pauper. It was first published serially in Century Magazine and, when it was finally published in book form, Pudd'nhead Wilson appeared as the main title; however, the "subtitles" make the entire title read: The Tragedy of Pudd'nhead Wilson and the Comedy of The Extraordinary Twins.

Twain's next venture was a work of straight fiction that he called Personal Recollections of Joan of Arc and dedicated to his wife. He had long said[where?] that this was the work that he was most proud of, despite the criticism that he received for it. The book had been a dream of his since childhood, and he claimed that he had found a manuscript detailing the life of Joan of Arc when he was an adolescent. This was another piece that he was convinced would save his publishing company. His financial adviser Henry Huttleston Rogers quashed that idea and got Twain out of that business altogether, but the book was published nonetheless.[citation needed]

To pay the bills and keep his business projects afloat, Twain had begun to write articles and commentary furiously, with diminishing returns, but it was not enough. He filed for bankruptcy in 1894. During this time of dire financial straits, he published several literary reviews in newspapers to help make ends meet. He famously derided James Fenimore Cooper in his article detailing Cooper's "Literary Offenses". He became an extremely outspoken critic of other authors and other critics; he suggested that, before praising Cooper's work, Thomas Lounsbury, Brander Matthews, and Wilkie Collins "ought to have read some of it".

George Eliot, Jane Austen, and Robert Louis Stevenson also fell under Twain's attack during this time period, beginning around 1890 and continuing until his death. He outlines what he considers to be "quality writing" in several letters and essays, in addition to providing a source for the "tooth and claw" style of literary criticism. He places emphasis on concision, utility of word choice, and realism; he complains, for example, that Cooper's Deerslayer purports to be realistic but has several shortcomings. Ironically, several of his own works were later criticized for lack of continuity (Adventures of Huckleberry Finn) and organization (Pudd'nhead Wilson).

Twain's wife died in 1904 while the couple were staying at the Villa di Quarto in Florence. After some time had passed he published some works that his wife, his de facto editor and censor throughout her married life, had looked down upon. The Mysterious Stranger is perhaps the best known, depicting various visits of Satan to earth. This particular work was not published in Twain's lifetime. His manuscripts included three versions, written between 1897 and 1905: the so-called Hannibal, Eseldorf, and Print Shop versions. The resulting confusion led to extensive publication of a jumbled version, and only recently have the original versions become available as Twain wrote them.

Twain's last work was his autobiography, which he dictated and thought would be most entertaining if he went off on whims and tangents in non-chronological order. Some archivists and compilers have rearranged the biography into a more conventional form, thereby eliminating some of Twain's humor and the flow of the book. The first volume of the autobiography, over 736 pages, was published by the University of California in November 2010, 100 years after his death, as Twain wished. It soon became an unexpected best-seller, making Twain one of a very few authors publishing new best-selling volumes in the 19th, 20th, and 21st centuries.

**Censorship**

Twain's works have been subjected to censorship efforts. According to Stuart (2013), "Leading these banning campaigns, generally, were religious organizations or individuals in positions of influence – not so much working librarians, who had been instilled with that American "library spirit" which honored intellectual freedom (within bounds of course)". In 1905, the Brooklyn Public Library banned both The Adventures of Huckleberry Finn and The Adventures of Tom Sawyer from the children's department because of their language.

### Views

Twain's views became more radical as he grew older. In a letter to friend and fellow writer William Dean Howells in 1887 he acknowledged that his views had changed and developed over his lifetime, referring to one of his favorite works:

When I finished Carlyle's French Revolution in 1871, I was a Girondin; every time I have read it since, I have read it differently – being influenced and changed, little by little, by life and environment ... and now I lay the book down once more, and recognize that I am a Sansculotte! And not a pale, characterless Sansculotte, but a Marat.

### Anti-imperialist

Before 1899, Twain was an ardent imperialist. In the late 1860s and early 1870s, he spoke out strongly in favor of American interests in the Hawaiian Islands. He said the war with Spain in 1898 was "the worthiest" war ever fought. In 1899, however, he reversed course. In the New York Herald, October 16, 1900, Twain describes his transformation and political awakening, in the context of the Philippine–American War, to anti-imperialism:

I wanted the American eagle to go screaming into the Pacific ... Why not spread its wings over the Philippines, I asked myself? ... I said to myself, Here are a people who have suffered for three centuries. We can make them as free as ourselves, give them a government and country of their own, put a miniature of the American Constitution afloat in the Pacific, start a brand new republic to take its place among the free nations of the world. It seemed to me a great task to which we had addressed ourselves.

But I have thought some more, since then, and I have read carefully the treaty of Paris [which ended the Spanish–American War], and I have seen that we do not intend to free, but to subjugate the people of the Philippines. We have gone there to conquer, not to redeem.

It should, it seems to me, be our pleasure and duty to make those people free, and let them deal with their own domestic questions in their own way. And so I am an anti-imperialist. I am opposed to having the eagle put its talons on any other land.

During the Boxer rebellion, Twain said that "the Boxer is a patriot. He loves his country better than he does the countries of other people. I wish him success."

From 1901, soon after his return from Europe, until his death in 1910, Twain was vice-president of the American Anti-Imperialist League, which opposed the annexation of the Philippines by the United States and had "tens of thousands of members". He wrote many political pamphlets for the organization. The Incident in the Philippines, posthumously published in 1924, was in response to the Moro Crater Massacre, in which six hundred Moros were killed. Many of his neglected and previously uncollected writings on anti-imperialism appeared for the first time in book form in 1992.

Twain was critical of imperialism in other countries as well. In Following the Equator, Twain expresses "hatred and condemnation of imperialism of all stripes". He was highly critical of European imperialists, such as Cecil Rhodes, who greatly expanded the British Empire, and Leopold II, King of the Belgians. King Leopold's Soliloquy is a stinging political satire about his private colony, the Congo Free State. Reports of outrageous exploitation and grotesque abuses led to widespread international protest in the early 1900s, arguably the first large-scale human rights movement. In the soliloquy, the King argues that bringing Christianity to the country outweighs a little starvation. Leopold's rubber gatherers were tortured, maimed and slaughtered until the movement forced Brussels to call a halt.

During the Philippine–American War, Twain wrote a short pacifist story titled The War Prayer, which makes the point that humanism and Christianity's preaching of love are incompatible with the conduct of war. It was submitted to Harper's Bazaar for publication, but on March 22, 1905, the magazine rejected the story as "not quite suited to a woman's magazine". Eight days later, Twain wrote to his friend Daniel Carter Beard, to whom he had read the story, "I don't think the prayer will be published in my time. None but the dead are permitted to tell the truth." Because he had an exclusive contract with Harper & Brothers, Twain could not publish The War Prayer elsewhere; it remained unpublished until 1923. It was republished as campaigning material by Vietnam War protesters.

Twain acknowledged that he had originally sympathized with the more moderate Girondins of the French Revolution and then shifted his sympathies to the more radical Sansculottes, indeed identifying himself as "a Marat" and writing that the Reign of Terror paled in comparison to the older terrors that preceded it. Twain supported the revolutionaries in Russia against the reformists, arguing that the Tsar must be got rid of by violent means, because peaceful ones would not work. He summed up his views of revolutions in the following statement:

I am said to be a revolutionist in my sympathies, by birth, by breeding and by principle. I am always on the side of the revolutionists, because there never was a revolution unless there were some oppressive and intolerable conditions against which to revolute.

**Civil rights**

Twain was an adamant supporter of the abolition of slavery and the emancipation of slaves, even going so far as to say, "Lincoln's Proclamation ... not only set the black slaves free, but set the white man free also". He argued that non-whites did not receive justice in the United States, once saying, "I have seen Chinamen abused and maltreated in all the mean, cowardly ways possible to the invention of a degraded nature ... but I never saw a Chinaman righted in a court of justice for wrongs thus done to him". He paid for at least one black person to attend Yale Law School and for another black person to attend a southern university to become a minister.

Twain's sympathetic views on race were not reflected in his early writings on American Indians. Of them, Twain wrote in 1870:

His heart is a cesspool of falsehood, of treachery, and of low and devilish instincts. With him, gratitude is an unknown emotion; and when one does him a kindness, it is safest to keep the face toward him, lest the reward be an arrow in the back. To accept of a favor from him is to assume a debt which you can never repay to his satisfaction, though you bankrupt yourself trying. The scum of the earth!

As counterpoint, Twain's essay on "The Literary Offenses of Fenimore Cooper" offers a much kinder view of Indians. "No, other Indians would have noticed these things, but Cooper's Indians never notice anything. Cooper thinks they are marvelous creatures for noticing, but he was almost always in error about his Indians. There was seldom a sane one among them." In his later travelogue Following the Equator (1897), Twain observes that in colonized lands all over the world, "savages" have always been wronged by "whites" in the most merciless ways, such as "robbery, humiliation, and slow, slow murder, through poverty and the white man's whiskey"; his conclusion is that "there are many humorous things in this world; among them the white man's notion that he is less savage than the other savages". In an expression that captures his East Indian experiences, he wrote, "So far as I am able to judge nothing has been left undone, either by man or Nature, to make India the most extraordinary country that the sun visits on his rounds. Where every prospect pleases, and only man is vile."

Twain was also a staunch supporter of women's rights and an active campaigner for women's suffrage. His "Votes for Women" speech, in which he pressed for the granting of voting rights to women, is considered one of the most famous in history.

Helen Keller benefited from Twain's support as she pursued her college education and publishing despite her disabilities and financial limitations. The two were friends for roughly 16 years.

Through Twain's efforts, the Connecticut legislature voted a pension for Prudence Crandall, since 1995 Connecticut's official heroine, for her efforts towards the education of African-American young ladies in Connecticut. Twain also offered to purchase for her use her former house in Canterbury, home of the Canterbury Female Boarding School, but she declined.

**Labor**

Twain wrote glowingly about unions in the river boating industry in Life on the Mississippi, which was read in union halls decades later. He supported the labor movement, especially one of the most important unions, the Knights of Labor. In a speech to them, he said:

Who are the oppressors? The few: the King, the capitalist, and a handful of other overseers and superintendents. Who are the oppressed? The many: the nations of the earth; the valuable personages; the workers; they that make the bread that the soft-handed and idle eat.

**Religion**

Twain was a Presbyterian. He was critical of organized religion and certain elements of Christianity through his later life. He wrote, for example, "Faith is believing what you know ain't so", and "If Christ were here now there is one thing he would not be – a Christian". With anti-Catholic sentiment rampant in 19th century America, Twain noted he was "educated to enmity toward everything that is Catholic". As an adult, he engaged in religious discussions and attended services, his theology developing as he wrestled with the deaths of loved ones and with his own mortality.

Twain generally avoided publishing his most controversial opinions on religion in his lifetime, and they are known from essays and stories that were published later. In the essay Three Statements of the Eighties in the 1880s, Twain stated that he believed in an almighty God, but not in any messages, revelations, holy scriptures such as the Bible, Providence, or retribution in the afterlife. He did state that "the goodness, the justice, and the mercy of God are manifested in His works", but also that "the universe is governed by strict and immutable laws", which determine "small matters", such as who dies in a pestilence. At other times, he wrote or spoke in ways that contradicted a strict deist view, for example, plainly professing a belief in Providence. In some later writings in the 1890s, he was less optimistic about the goodness of God, observing that "if our Maker is all-powerful for good or evil, He is not in His right mind". At other times, he conjectured sardonically that perhaps God had created the world with all its tortures for some purpose of His own, but was otherwise indifferent to humanity, which was too petty and insignificant to deserve His attention anyway.

In 1901, Twain criticized the actions of the missionary Dr. William Scott Ament (1851–1909) because Ament and other missionaries had collected indemnities from Chinese subjects in the aftermath of the Boxer Uprising of 1900. Twain's response to hearing of Ament's methods was published in the North American Review in February 1901: To the Person Sitting in Darkness, and deals with examples of imperialism in China, South Africa, and with the U.S. occupation of the Philippines. A subsequent article, "To My Missionary Critics" published in The North American Review in April 1901, unapologetically continues his attack, but with the focus shifted from Ament to his missionary superiors, the American Board of Commissioners for Foreign Missions.

After his death, Twain's family suppressed some of his work that was especially irreverent toward conventional religion, including Letters from the Earth, which was not published until his daughter Clara reversed her position in 1962 in response to Soviet propaganda about the withholding. The anti-religious The Mysterious Stranger was published in 1916. Little Bessie, a story ridiculing Christianity, was first published in the 1972 collection Mark Twain's Fables of Man.

He raised money to build a Presbyterian Church in Nevada in 1864.

Twain created a reverent portrayal of Joan of Arc, a subject over which he had obsessed for forty years, studied for a dozen years and spent two years writing about. In 1900 and again in 1908 he stated, "I like Joan of Arc best of all my books, it is the best".

Those who knew Twain well late in life recount that he dwelt on the subject of the afterlife, his daughter Clara saying: "Sometimes he believed death ended everything, but most of the time he felt sure of a life beyond."

Twain's frankest views on religion appeared in his final work Autobiography of Mark Twain, the publication of which started in November 2010, 100 years after his death. In it, he said:

There is one notable thing about our Christianity: bad, bloody, merciless, money-grabbing, and predatory as it is – in our country particularly and in all other Christian countries in a somewhat modified degree – it is still a hundred times better than the Christianity of the Bible, with its prodigious crime – the invention of Hell. Measured by our Christianity of to-day, bad as it is, hypocritical as it is, empty and hollow as it is, neither the Deity nor his Son is a Christian, nor qualified for that moderately high place. Ours is a terrible religion. The fleets of the world could swim in spacious comfort in the innocent blood it has spilled.

Twain was a Freemason. He belonged to Polar Star Lodge No. 79 A.F.&A.M., based in St. Louis. He was initiated an Entered Apprentice on May 22, 1861, passed to the degree of Fellow Craft on June 12, and raised to the degree of Master Mason on July 10.

Twain visited Salt Lake City for two days and met there members of The Church of Jesus Christ of Latter-day Saints. They also gave him a Book of Mormon. He later wrote in Roughing It about that book:

The book seems to be merely a prosy detail of imaginary history, with the Old Testament for a model; followed by a tedious plagiarism of the New Testament.

**Vivisection**

Twain was opposed to the vivisection practices of his day. His objection was not on a scientific basis but rather an ethical one. He specifically cited the pain caused to the animal as his basis of his opposition:

I am not interested to know whether Vivisection produces results that are profitable to the human race or doesn't. ... The pains which it inflicts upon unconsenting animals is the basis of my enmity towards it, and it is to me sufficient justification of the enmity without looking further.

**Pen names**

Twain used different pen names before deciding on "Mark Twain". He signed humorous and imaginative sketches as "Josh" until 1863. Additionally, he used the pen name "Thomas Jefferson Snodgrass" for a series of humorous letters.

He maintained that his primary pen name came from his years working on Mississippi riverboats, where two fathoms, a depth indicating water safe for the passage of boat, was a measure on the sounding line. Twain is an archaic term for "two", as in "The veil of the temple was rent in twain." The riverboatman's cry was "mark twain" or, more fully, "by the mark twain", meaning "according to the mark [on the line], [the depth is] two [fathoms]", that is, "The water is 12 feet (3.7 m) deep and it is safe to pass."

Twain said that his famous pen name was not entirely his invention. In Life on the Mississippi, he wrote:

Captain Isaiah Sellers was not of literary turn or capacity, but he used to jot down brief paragraphs of plain practical information about the river, and sign them "MARK TWAIN", and give them to the New Orleans Picayune. They related to the stage and condition of the river, and were accurate and valuable; ... At the time that the telegraph brought the news of his death, I was on the Pacific coast. I was a fresh new journalist, and needed a nom de guerre; so I confiscated the ancient mariner's discarded one, and have done my best to make it remain what it was in his hands – a sign and symbol and warrant that whatever is found in its company may be gambled on as being the petrified truth; how I have succeeded, it would not be modest in me to say.

Twain's story about his pen name has been questioned by some with the suggestion that "mark twain" refers to a running bar tab that Twain would regularly incur while drinking at John Piper's saloon in Virginia City, Nevada. Samuel Clemens himself responded to this suggestion by saying, "Mark Twain was the nom de plume of one Captain Isaiah Sellers, who used to write river news over it for the New Orleans Picayune. He died in 1869 and as he could no longer need that signature, I laid violent hands upon it without asking permission of the proprietor's remains. That is the history of the nom de plume I bear."

In his autobiography, Twain writes further of Captain Sellers' use of "Mark Twain":

I was a cub pilot on the Mississippi River then, and one day I wrote a rude and crude satire which was leveled at Captain Isaiah Sellers, the oldest steamboat pilot on the Mississippi River, and the most respected, esteemed, and revered. For many years he had occasionally written brief paragraphs concerning the river and the changes which it had undergone under his observation during fifty years, and had signed these paragraphs "Mark Twain" and published them in the St. Louis and New Orleans journals. In my satire I made rude game of his reminiscences. It was a shabby poor performance, but I didn't know it, and the pilots didn't know it. The pilots thought it was brilliant. They were jealous of Sellers, because when the gray-heads among them pleased their vanity by detailing in the hearing of the younger craftsmen marvels which they had seen in the long ago on the river, Sellers was always likely to step in at the psychological moment and snuff them out with wonders of his own which made their small marvels look pale and sick. However, I have told all about this in "Old Times on the Mississippi." The pilots handed my extravagant satire to a river reporter, and it was published in the New Orleans True Delta. That poor old Captain Sellers was deeply wounded. He had never been held up to ridicule before; he was sensitive, and he never got over the hurt which I had wantonly and stupidly inflicted upon his dignity. I was proud of my performance for a while, and considered it quite wonderful, but I have changed my opinion of it long ago. Sellers never published another paragraph nor ever used his nom de guerre again.

**Legacy and depictions**

**Trademark white suit**

While Twain is often depicted wearing a white suit, modern representations suggesting that he wore them throughout his life are unfounded. Evidence suggests that Twain began wearing white suits on the lecture circuit, after the death of his wife Olivia ("Livy") in 1904. However, there is also evidence showing him wearing a white suit before 1904. In 1882, he sent a photograph of himself in a white suit to 18-year-old Edward W. Bok, later publisher of the Ladies Home Journal, with a handwritten dated note. The white suit did eventually become his trademark, as illustrated in anecdotes about this eccentricity (such as the time he wore a white summer suit to a Congressional hearing during the winter). McMasters' The Mark Twain Encyclopedia states that Twain did not wear a white suit in his last three years, except at one banquet speech.

In his autobiography, Twain writes of his early experiments with wearing white out-of-season:

Next after fine colors, I like plain white. One of my sorrows, when the summer ends, is that I must put off my cheery and comfortable white clothes and enter for the winter into the depressing captivity of the shapeless and degrading black ones. It is mid-October now, and the weather is growing cold up here in the New Hampshire hills, but it will not succeed in freezing me out of these white garments, for here the neighbors are few, and it is only of crowds that I am afraid. (Source: Wikipedia)

Lightning Source UK Ltd.
Milton Keynes UK
UKHW010830300420
362537UK00005B/89

## *Other Travel Guide Books by Passport to European Travel Guides*

Top 10 Travel Guide to Italy

Florence, Italy

Rome, Italy

Venice, Italy

Paris, France

Provence & the French Riviera, France

Top 10 Travel Guide to France

London, England

Barcelona, Spain

Amsterdam, Netherlands

Santorini, Greece

Greece & the Greek Islands

Berlin, Germany

Munich, Germany

Vienna, Austria

Istanbul, Turkey

Budapest, Hungary

Prague, Czech Republic

Brussels, Belgium

*"You may have the universe if I may have Italy."*

—*Giuseppe Verdi*

# Table of Contents

Map of Naples & the Amalfi Coast..........................7
Introduction: How to Use This Guide.......................9
City Snapshot................................................11
Before You Go...............................................13
Getting in the Mood
   • What to Read......................................19
   • What to Watch....................................19

Local Tourist Information..................................21
About the Airports..........................................21
How Long is the Flight?....................................21
Overview of Naples & the Amalfi Coast..................23
   ★ Insider Tips for Tourists! ★..............................25
Italian Phrases For Emergencies..........................32
Climate and Best Times to Travel........................36
Tours
   • By Bike...............................................38
   • By Boat..............................................39
   • By Bus...............................................40
   • Special Interest or Walking Tours..................40

★ 5 Days in Naples & the Amalfi Coast—Itinerary! ★
   • Day 1................................................43
   • Day 2................................................46
   • Day 3................................................48
   • Day 4................................................50

- Day 5.................................................52

Best Places For Travelers on a Budget
- Bargain Italian Sleeps......................................55
- Bargain Italian Eats............................................57

Best Places For Ultimate Luxury
- Luxury Italian Sleeps........................................59
- Luxury Italian Eats............................................61

Naples & Amalfi Coast Nightlife
- Great Bars..........................................................63
- Great Clubs........................................................64
- Great Live Music...............................................65
- Great Theater.....................................................66

Conclusion.................................................................67

About the Authors.....................................................68

# • Map of Naples & the Amalfi Coast •

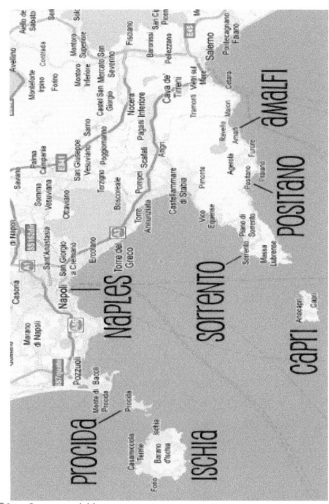

© Image Courtesy: www.italylogue.com

# • Introduction •

**N**aples, Italy. Napoli. The birthplace of pizza! Need we go on?

**Italy's gorgeous Amalfi coastline** has quickly become one of the world's leading vacation destinations—a fabulous stretch of coastline in southern Italy, frequently dotted by the **impressive yachts** of everyone from Hollywood celebrities to foreign dignitaries who frequently cruise along **Amalfi's beautiful shores.**

**With cultural and historical** highlights such as the ancient ruins of **Pompeii**, to the striking architecture and cobblestoned streets of **Sorrento**, this region of the world has much to offer visitors. **A jaunt through any of the brimming** Italian villages of Naples and the Amalfi Coast can mean overindulging in Neapolitan pizzas, delicious pastas, rich and flavorful Italian coffees, not to mention mouthwatering gelato!

**In this 5-day guide to Italy's Naples and Amalfi Coast,** you'll find a variety of our top recommendations and helpful tips to prepare you for having the best travel experience in Italy! **Read over the insider tips** carefully and familiarize yourself with the information on preparing for your trip. **Every traveler** has different preferences, and we've included a wide range of recommendations to suit all tastes and budgets.

**You're welcome** to follow our detailed **5-day itinerary** to the letter, or you can **mix and match** the activities at your own discretion.

**Most importantly**, we know you're sure to have a great time experiencing this wonderful region of Italy!

Enjoy!

**The Passport to European Travel Guides Team**

# • City Snapshot •

**Language:** Italian

**Local Airports:** Naples International Airport (Italian: Aeroporto Internazionale di Napoli) (NAP)

**Currency:** Euro | € (EUR)

**Country Code:** 39

**Emergencies:** 112 (any emergency within the European Union), 113 (police), 115 (fire department), 118 (first aid, EMS). The emergency calls at 112 are answered in Italian, English, French, and German.

# • Before You Go... •

## ✓ Have a Passport

**If you don't already have one**, you'll need to apply for a passport in your home country a good two months before you intend to travel, to avoid cutting it too close. **You'll need to find a local passport agency**, complete an application, take fresh photos of yourself, have at least one form of ID and pay an application fee. **If you're in a hurry**, you can usually expedite the application for a 2-3 week turnaround at an additional cost.

## ✓ Need a Visa?

**Using the following website**, by entering your nationality, your country of residence, your stay duration and reason for visit, you will immediately find out whether or not a visa is required in your case:
http://vistoperitalia.esteri.it/home/en
(**American and Canadian citizens** are not required to apply for a visa for Italy if they are planning to stay for **less than 90 days.**)

## ✓ Healthcare

Italy ranks among the **World Health Organization's top 10** countries for quality health services. Their national health care system provides free or very low cost healthcare. However, if you're not an Italian resident, payment will typically be expected at the time services are rendered.

**When visiting from outside Europe**, it's a good idea to buy supplemental medical insurance to ensure you'll be covered for all costs while in Italy. And remember to **carry your health insurance information** with you at all times when traveling.

**Many Italian doctors** speak decent English, so communication during emergencies should not be a problem.

## ✓ Set the Date

**Setting the date** for your travel to Naples or the Amalfi Coast should be based on your budget, and on what you would like to experience during the trip. For better rates, we recommend you book everything — flights, hotels, tours, train and bus passes, etc. — **as far in advance as possible**.

**We think the best time to visit** Naples and the Amalfi Coast is between **April and May** in the spring, and **September to October** in the fall. The weather is best in these months, with nice, mild temperatures.

We recommend **avoiding the summertime** (June & August) if at all possible — even Italians do — because the summer months are very hot; some would even say stifling and unpleasant.

**Winter is a particularly popular** tourist season in this region of Italy, especially around Christmas and New

Year's Eve. Naples is known for having some of the best fireworks shows in the country!

## ✓ Pack

• **When planning** your trip to Italy, you should consider packing only the essentials appropriate for the season in which you'll be traveling. By far, the most important thing to pack is a good pair of **walking shoes** (water-resistant if you're traveling in colder months; comfortable, light sandals or sneakers to walk good distances in the warmer weather).

• We don't advise bringing **completely new shoes** on your trip — test them before you have to use them. You'll be doing a lot of walking in these cities, so it's absolutely crucial to have the best, most comfortable shoes with you!

• If you're planning on visiting the beautiful cathedrals of Italy, bring **clothes that appropriately cover** your shoulders and legs.

• **In the colder months**, bring a **warm sweater**, clothes that you can layer, and a **rain jacket or umbrella.** Don't forget **beachwear, sunscreen, sunglasses, and a hat.**

• **A backpack** can be handy during the day when you go out sightseeing and collecting souvenirs, particularly when getting on and off buses, boats, trains or trams.

• **If you don't speak Italian**, be sure to pack a good **Italian phrase guide** to bring along with you. You'll find people a lot friendlier toward you if you don't go around assuming they speak your language.

• **Hand sanitizer** is always great to have along with you when traveling.

• A simple **first aid kit** is always a good idea to have in your luggage, just in case.

• As far as must-have electronics, don't forget that **Europe uses 220 volts**, so bring a **power converter** and **extended battery case** for your smart phones, tablets or laptops.

• Make **copies of your travel documents and your passport** and email them to yourself before your trip — this can prevent lots of hassle if you happen to lose your documents.

• And don't forget any **medication** that you take regularly. Make sure to bring enough of it with you and bring **a note from your doctor** if you're suffering from a condition that others need to be aware of. If you have lots of medication, ask an Italian friend (or pay someone) to translate your doctor's note into Italian, print it out and carry it with you in your wallet or purse.

• Be sure to **leave expensive jewels and high-priced electronics at home**. Like most major cities and tourist attractions, thieves and pickpockets abound in tourist areas. Avoid making yourself a target.

• Bring one or two **reusable shopping bags** for trips to the grocery store and for carrying souvenirs home!

## ✓ Phone Home

**How will you call** home from Italy? Does your cell phone company offer service while abroad? **What are their rates?**

There are many ways to **call home** from Italy that are inexpensive or completely free.

You may also **sign up for roaming or Internet hotspots** through your own cell phone provider. You can also use Skype, WhatsApp, Viper, or many other voice-over IP providers that are entirely free.

**Other options** are to buy an **Italian phone chip** for your phone (which also gives you an Italian phone number), purchase **calling codes** before you leave home, or you can buy **calling cards** or **prepaid cell phones** once you arrive in Italy.

## ✓ Currency Exchange

**Italy uses the euro** (€) as its currency (the same as most of Western and Central Europe). Check out the currency exchange rates prior to your trip. You can do so online using the following or many other online currency exchange calculators, or through your local bank: http://www.xe.com/currencyconverter

**Make sure your bank knows** you'll be traveling abroad. This way you avoid having your foreign country transactions flagged and declined, which can be extremely inconvenient.

## ✓ Contact Your Embassy

**In the unfortunate event** that you should lose your passport or be victimized while away, **your country's embassy** will be able to help you. Be sure to give your itinerary and contact information to a close **friend or family member**, then also contact your embassy with your emergency contact information before you leave.

## ✓ Your Mail

Ask a neighbor to **check your mailbox** while you're away or visit your local post office and request a hold. **Overflowing mailboxes** are a dead giveaway that no one's home.

# • Getting in the Mood •

Here are a few great books and films (set in Naples or on the Amalfi Coast) that we recommend you read and watch in preparation for your trip to these exciting locales!

## What to Read:

**A great contemporary mystery** novel set in Naples is Michael Dibdin's ***Cosi Fan Tutti***. It's about a cop stationed in Naples who helps out a wealthy widow, only to become involved in a murder case himself!

**Another great read** is a bestseller called, ***Last Voyage of the Valentina*** by Santa Montefiore. An English woman becomes inspired to travel to the Amalfi Coast to discover the truth her father hides about her late mother.

## What to Watch:

Roberto Rossellini's ***Journey to Italy*** stars the legendary Ingrid Bergman and is considered one of the most influential films in Italian Cinema. Naples is the gorgeous backdrop for the dramatic story of an English couple's declining marriage. This is a classic you don't want to miss!

Another great movie set on the Amalfi Coast is 2004's ***A Good Woman***, starring Scarlett Johansson and Helen

Hunt. Shot on location in Italy, the coast serves as the backdrop for some dramatic man stealing! This is a remake of the famed Oscar Wilde play.

## • Local Tourist Information •

**Tourist bureaus** can be found at the airport in Naples as well as any train or bus station along the Amalfi Coast.

## • About the Airports •

**Naples International Airport** (Italian: Aeroporto Internazionale di Napoli) (NAP) is located in the Capodichino district of Naples and is the airport that serves this region of Italy. It is approximately 40 miles (60 km) from the Amalfi Coast.

**The airport's website is:**
http://www.aeroportodinapoli.it

## • How Long is the Flight? •

• **The flight to Naples from New York City** is approx. 11 hours

• **From Los Angeles** approx. 15 hours

• **From Toronto** approx. 11 hours

• **From Paris** approx. 2 hours

• **From London** approx. 2.5 hours

- **From Moscow** approx. 4 hours
- **From Beijing** approx. 13 hours
- **From Hong Kong** approx. 16.5 hours
- **From Cape Town** approx. 17.5 hours
- **From Sydney** approx. 24 hours

# • Overview of Naples & the Amalfi Coast •

**The third largest city in Italy**, Naples (Napoli in Italian) rests about two hours south of Rome and is today divided into 10 individual municipalities or districts. As one of the country's oldest cities, there's no limit to the amazing architecture and distinctive tradition to be discovered and explored in Naples.

**Italy's Amalfi Coast** is about 40 miles south of Naples (roughly an hour by train) and runs for 31 magnificent miles along the Sorrentine Peninsula. There is no location lacking in magnificent views!

**The coastline cities** of Amalfi, Positano, Sorrento, Salerno and others, feature colorful fishing villages full of stunning cliffside houses that are sure to completely win your heart...unless the indigo seawaters and sandy beaches grab it first!

**Exciting hot spots** await you all around Naples, or from any of the towns along the Amalfi Coast. A jaunt to explore the ruins of **Pompeii** or the islands of **Capri and Ischia** are just a day trip away once you're on the ground in Naples!

**So smile.** You're going to Italy!

# • Insider Tips For Tourists •

## Etiquette

**Coffee Etiquette:** As you may know, Italians are very serious about coffee and there are certain "rules" for ordering and drinking it.

**Breakfast often consists** of a pastry and a cappuccino, or sometimes a shot of espresso. When away from home, breakfast is almost always eaten standing in a local bar, so don't expect long, leisurely breakfasts in Italy. And espresso isn't sipped—just downed in one big gulp.

In Italy, **cappuccino** is generally a **morning drink**. Italians don't usually have it anytime after noon. So if you ask for a cappuccino with dinner, or even with your pasta at lunch, don't be surprised if your request is met with a queer look. A post-dinner espresso, however, is perfectly normal and even a favorite of locals.

**Dinner Etiquette:** In Italy, guests are expected to be at least fifteen minutes late for dinner reservations. Menus are for tourists. You'll hear local patrons just ask for the daily specials. Locals usually have dinner late, around 9:00 pm, but not to worry, most restaurants keep traditional hours to accommodate tourists.

**Personal Space Etiquette:** In contrast to Western culture, Italians tend to be much more touchy-feely and not as observant of personal space. Don't be surprised if they hug or kiss you in a first greeting, rather than offer a mere handshake.

**Pedestrian Etiquette:** Italians typically walk fast, especially in places like Venice, so whenever you stop, be sure you're not blocking the bridge or walkway. **Walk on the right-hand side,** and ensure people can **pass by on the left**.

**Traffic Etiquette:** Traffic in Italy can be a nightmare for tourists. Cars won't stop for you unless you're at a **designated crosswalk** or have a green light. **Pedestrians** always get the right of way at crosswalks, but proceed with caution when driving or crossing the street—there are plenty of bad drivers in every city.

**Picnic Etiquette:** Be sure not to set up shop near tourist attractions unless there are designated areas for doing so. Picnic on the beach or in a park. Avoid laying out a picnic near churches, doorways, monuments, bridges, etc.

**Soccer Etiquette:** Just about all Italian men are passionate about soccer and their favorite teams. **Be careful not to offend**—try not to yawn when the topic of soccer comes up...yet again. We recommend educating yourself about European soccer before venturing out to local bars during the soccer season, which is usually August thru May.

## Time Zone

Naples and the Amalfi Coast are in the **Central European Time Zone** (UTC + 1:00). There is a six-hour time difference between New York City and Italy (Italy is ahead). When it's 8:00 am in New York City, it's 2:00 pm in Naples and on the Amalfi Coast.

**The format for abbreviating dates** in Europe is different from the US. They use: **day/month/year**. So for example, August 23, 2035 is written in Europe as 23 August 2035, or 23/8/35.

## Saving Time & Money

• **To save money on airfare, it may be best to fly into Rome's airport** and take the train to Naples. Flying into Rome is usually less expensive than flying into most of the other airports in Italy. **Compare fares** and see if you'd save.

• Make sure you **keep yourself hydrated** to avoid becoming overly tired, **plan your routes** in advance and pace yourself.

• Wherever you're staying, you can **save on buying daily meals** by finding a local market that offers fresh produce, seafood, street food, etc., and opting for **picnics** on the beach or in the park, or for having **quick meals** in your room.

- Take advantage of the **complimentary breakfast** at your hotel and **eat well** so you start the morning with enough energy to fuel a long day of sightseeing.

- **To avoid high hotel and restaurants rates** in Naples or any of the high tourism towns on the Amalfi Coast, **avoid staying in the city center**. Particularly in Naples where there's an abundance of public transportation options for getting downtown from wherever you choose to stay. However, should you opt to stay in one of the hotels in the historic city center, the **earlier in advance** you can book your stay, the less expensive it will be.

- **To save on buying daily meals**, you can enjoy a truly genuine European outdoor market experience at **La Pignasecca** in Naples, a great market that offers fresh produce, delicious seafood, handmade clothing and shoes, and lots more. They open around 8:00 am and close early in the afternoon. You can stroll through and pick up snacks for a nice picnic lunch and/or dinner—**much less expensive** and more intimate than eating in cafés and restaurants for every meal. (**La Pignasecca** is located at: Via Pignasecca, 80134, Naples, Italy. Your hotel should have no problem pointing you in the right direction.)

## Tipping

Tipping is not required in Italy. **Most restaurant checks** will already include a service upcharge, but **as a tourist**, you're expected to tip waiters, bellmen, chambermaids, restroom attendants, hair stylists, etc., for **ex-**

cellent service. If you take a cab and the driver helped you with heavy luggage, it's **courteous** to tip a few euros.

Most Italians will only tip (about 10%) when service is exceptional.

## When You Have to Go

*Posso usare il bagno?* Means: May I use the restroom? *Dov'è il bagno?* Means: Where is the bathroom? Learn these two very important phrases, as you will most likely need them while sightseeing through Italy.

**Going to the restroom** in a **foreign country** can be a hilarious—or even traumatic—experience if you're not familiar with how things work there. **Try not to use too much toilet paper** in restrooms unless you're told it's okay to do so, but if you're unsure, **do not flush it down the toilet**. Instead use a bag that you tie up and dispose of when finished. The old Italian toilet and sewer system simply cannot handle much toilet paper and can quickly back up and create quite a mess.

**And again, remember** to leave a tip for **restroom attendants.**

## Taxes

**The Value Added Tax** (or VAT) is a consumption tax. The standard rate in Italy is 22%. Reduced VAT rates apply for pharmaceuticals, passenger transport, admission to cultural and entertainment events, hotels, restaurants (10%) and on foodstuffs, medical and books (4%). The Italian VAT is part of the European Union's value added tax system.

Visitors from outside Europe may be eligible for a **VAT refund** if certain criteria are met: 1) you do not live in Europe 2) you must be leaving within 3 months of the purchase 3) purchase must be made in a shop or business that participates in the Retail Export Scheme or Tax Free Shopping program 4) purchases must meet the minimum of about €155 spent in one shop at one time.

**To obtain a VAT refund**, ask the store or shop attendant for the **appropriate form** (participating shops usually have some sort of signage, but if not, just ask). You will need to present the form to customs at the airport for processing.

## Phone Calls

Italy's **country code** is 39.

**When calling home** from Italy, first dial 00. You will then hear a tone. Then dial the country code (1 for the U.S. and Canada, 44 for the UK, 61 for Australia, 7 for Russia, 81 for Japan, and 86 for China), then the area code without any initial 0, then the actual phone number.

## Electricity

**Electricity in Italy**, as in the rest of Europe, uses **220-240 volts** alternating at 50 cycles per second (by comparison, the U.S. uses 110 volts, alternating at 60 cycles per second.) Not only are the voltages and frequencies **different in Europe**, but the socket plugs are as well. **So we must stress** that travelers from outside of Europe need to bring along a **power and plug converter** to ensure that your phones, tablets, hairdryers, curling irons, laptops, etc., will work while you're abroad — and also won't be fried by the higher voltage they weren't built to handle.

## In Emergencies

You should keep the following phone numbers handy: **112 (emergency), 113 (police), 115 (fire department), 118 (first aid, EMS)**. The emergency calls at 112 are answered in English, Italian, French, and German.

**In case of an accident or life-threatening medical problem**, go or ask to be taken straight to a hospital. For serious conditions (stroke, heart attack, car accident with injuries), call an ambulance. If you don't have any other emergency numbers handy, you can always call 112, the European Union's universal emergency number for ambulance, fire department or the police.

**For minor health issues**, seek out a **farmacia** (signs have a green

cross). The opening hours of an Italian pharmacy are typically 9:00 am – 1:00 pm and 4:00 – 7:30 or 8:00 pm, Monday thru Friday, and on Saturday mornings. Outside of these hours, there is always **at least one pharmacy** on duty in each town, and its address is usually posted in the windows of all pharmacies in the area.

## Italian Phrases For Emergencies:

| I don't understand. | Non capisco. |
| --- | --- |
| Do you speak English? | Parla Inglese? |
| Where is the bathroom? | Dov'è il bagno? |
| Help! | Aiuto! |
| I don't speak Italian. | Non parlo Italiano. |
| I don't feel well. | Non me senti bene. |
| I need a doctor! | Ho bisogno di un dottore medico! |
| It's an emergency! | E un'emergenza! |
| There's a fire! | C'e un incedio! |

# Holidays

The following days are public holidays in Italy (and specifically in Naples):

| January 1 | New Year's Day | *Capodanno* |
|---|---|---|
| January 6 | Epiphany | *Epifania* |
| Monday after Easter | Easter Monday | *Lunedì dell'Angelo*, *Lunedì in Albis* or more commonly *Pasquetta* |
| April 25 | Liberation Day (from Nazi Germany) | *Festa della Liberazione* |
| May 1 | International Workers' Day | *Festa del Lavoro* (or*Festa dei Lavoratori*) |
| June 2 | Republic Day | *Festa della Repubblica* |
| August 15 | Assumption Day | *Ferragosto* and*Assunta* |
| September 19 | Feast of St. Januarius | *Naples Holiday* |
| November 1 | All Saints' Day | *Tutti i santi* (or*Ognissanti*) |
| December | Immaculate | *Immacolata Concezione* (or just*Immacola-* |

| 8 | Conception | *ta*) |
| December 25 | Christmas Day | *Natale* |
| December 26 | St. Stephen's Day | *Santo Stefano* |

## Hours of Operation

**Banks** are usually open between 8:30 am – 1:30 pm and 2:45 pm – 3:45 pm on weekdays. You may find some in tourist areas that stay open later.

**Stores and shops** typically open from 10:00 am – 7:00 pm, many with a long lunch break in between, anywhere from 1:00 pm – 3:30 pm, especially in the smaller towns.

Many **grocery stores** are closed on Sundays.

**Post offices** are typically open Monday–Saturday 8:00 am – 2:00 pm. Local newsstands will also sell stamps.

**Museum hours** in Italy can vary depending on the season (some of the more prominent museums stay open really late during the summer months). Many important national museums are closed one day a week, usually Mondays. **Always check ahead** to avoid wasting your time and being disappointed to show up and find them closed.

Most **gas stations** are open Monday through Saturday (most are closed on Sundays), and most close for lunch during the week (typically 1:00 pm – 3:00 pm). **Highway** gas stations usually stay open 24 hours.

Most **churches** open 7-8:00 am until noon or 12:30 pm; close for two or more hours, then re-open until 7-8:00 pm or later. **Major cathedrals and basilicas are open all day.** Visiting a church during mass is frowned upon.

# Money

**As mentioned**, the currency in Italy is the **euro** (€). Check out the currency exchange rates prior to your trip, online or through your bank. To obtain euros, we recommend waiting until you get to Italy and using the local ATMs.

**Some places** in Italy may accept U.S. dollars, but not many, and the exchange rate will usually be higher.

We also recommend simply **using your credit cards** for good exchange rates on purchases, but watch for **unnecessary fees.** When using your credit cards, always choose to **pay in euros** vs. dollars if you're given the option. Paying in dollars will usually cost you more in fees.

Almost no one uses **traveler's checks** anymore, so we don't recommend them. There are many easier and safer ways to handle money while traveling. Unless it cannot be avoided, **never carry more than €200 on you at a time,** in case of theft. It's easy to simply withdraw cash from the many ATMs in Italy or use your credit cards.

## Climate and Best Times to Travel

**We think the best time to visit** Naples and the Amalfi Coast is in the spring, between **April and May,** or in fall, between **September and October**. The weather is best in these months, with nice, **mild temperatures.**

We recommend **avoiding June & August** if at all possible — the summer months are very hot.

**Winter is particularly popular** for tourism in this part of Italy, especially around Christmas and New Year's Eve. Naples is known for having some of the best fireworks shows in the country!

## Transportation

**Naples is a major hub** and has good public transportation, including trams, a large network of buses, a subway system, funiculars, and a suburban train line (the Ferrovia Circumvesuviana) that will get you to any part of the region you wish to go.

**The main forms** of public transport serving the Amalfi Coast are **Sita coaches and ferries** (Metro del Mare) in the summertime. Most travelers opt to get around by ferry since it's faster and charmingly scenic!

**Tickets for the bus**, train or tram must be purchased before boarding. Most bus stops will not have a ticket machine on site. You can also buy tickets for any form of public transportation at metro stations, newsstands, bars or local stores that typically have signs that read: "Sali e Tabacchi."

**If you are planning** to use public transportation on a Sunday, be sure to purchase your tickets beforehand to avoid having to locate an open shop on a Sunday.

# Driving

**Since Naples and the Amalfi Coast** has such an excellent public transportation system, we don't recommend driving unless you're familiar with the area and have actually driven in Italy before. **Renting cars** is expensive and quite complicated, even for locals! Also, parking can be difficult to find and also pricey.

However, if you do end up opting to drive, please be sure you study the **traffic regulations** and print out your driving routes; or ensure your rental car has an English-language GPS you know how to use before you enter the Italian roadways.

# • Tours •

There are many great tours in this region of Italy. We feature our personal favorites below. We encourage you to try a few different ones — **by bike, by boat or on foot** — that way you can experience the country from a wonderful variety of perspectives!

**Be sure to call ahead and check websites** for pricing and other tour details, as these are subject to change.

## By Bike

**Cycling is a great**, immediate way to explore many of the beautiful places on the coast. We think **Cycling Amalfi Coast** offers the best guided half-day and full-day biking tours of the Amalfi Coast! For a more leisurely time, go with the full-day tours, they're designed to maximize your enjoyment of the coast's gorgeous panoramic views.

**Cycling Amalfi Coast**
**Address:** Piazza dello Spirito Santo 12, 84011, Amalfi
**Phone Number:** +39 327 851 5500
http://www.cyclingamalfi.com/en

**BikeTours.com** also does enjoyable cycling tours of the **Amalfi Coast and the Gulf of Naples.** They offer a nice combination bike and boat tour as well. Both are a real treat and never disappoint!

**BikeTours.com**
**Phone Number:** 1-877-462-2423
http://www.biketours.com/Italy/amalfi-coast-bike-and-boat

# By Boat

**Our top recommendation** for the best boat tour experience is with **Capitano Ago!** They promise to make your Italian holiday unique and memorable for the best value around. Check out their wide range of options, from private boat tours or rentals, to fishing tours and group excursions to Amalfi, Capri, Sorrento, Pompeii and more!

**Capitano Ago**
**Address:** Via Marina Grande, 92, 80067, Sorrento
**Phone Number:** +39 392 272 8910
http://www.capitanoago.com

**The Viator** also offers a variety of **day trip tours** from Naples to the Amalfi Coast. You can visit Positano, Pompeii, Sorrento, Ravello, and even the nearby island of Capri!

**The Viator's Amalfi Coast From Naples**
**Phone Number:** 1-888-651-9785
http://www.viator.com/Naples-tourism/Amalfi-Coast-from-Naples-tours-tickets/d508-t697

## By Bus

If you're looking for a fantastic and **comfortable bus tour** of the city of Naples, **City Sightseeing Napoli** is our favorite — prepare to be amazed!

**City Sightseeing Napoli**
**Phone Number:** +39 335 780 3812
http://www.napoli.city-sightseeing.it/eng/index.htm

For a more intimate road experience, **take a car tour** for four with **Get Your Guide's Full-Day Tour Along the Amalfi Coast!** They'll pick you up from your hotel in Naples and a personal tour guide will spend the day introducing you to the captivating scenery that is Italy's beautiful Amalfi Coast!

**Get Your Guide — Full-Day Tour Along the Amalfi Coast**
**Phone Number**: 1-866-941-3799
http://www.getyourguide.com/naples-l162/from-naples-full-day-tour-along-the-amalfi-coast-t46524

## Try Special Interest or Walking Tours

Looking forward to indulging in **delicious, mouth-watering Italian cuisine?** We recommend the **Viator's Sorrento Small Group Food Walking Tour!** You take a stroll with a knowledgeable local guide through the charming Neapolitan town of Sorrento, stopping at several restaurants and eateries for a sample of their yummy dishes!

**Sorrento Small Group Food Walking Tour**
**Phone Number:** 1-888-651-9785
http://www.viator.com/tours/Sorrento/Sorrento-Small-Group-Food-Walking-Tour/d947-6266FOOD

**If you're interested** in touring the ancient ruins of **Pompeii**, we highly recommend a guided tour. There are several available, but our favorite is **Tours of Capri's Ancient Pompeii Guided Tour.** It's a very popular tour, so Tours of Capri recommends booking well in advance.

**Tours of Capri: Ancient Pompeii Guided Tour**
**Phone Number:** +39 338 282 4366
http://www.toursofcapri.com/pompeiitour.html

**Another lovely day trip** option would be to the magical island of **Capri**, with a magical walking tour of the island! Capri is located in the beautiful Gulf of Naples. A magical day awaits with Tours of Capri's **Capri Island Guided Tour!**

**Tours of Capri: Capri Island Guided Tour**
**Phone Number:** +39 338 282 4366
http://www.toursofcapri.com/capriislandtour.html

**How about an underground tour of Naples?** Napoli Sotterranea offers a really interesting group tour, **Naples Underground**, that takes you more than 130 feet below the ground of the Historic Center of Naples to uncover the secrets of times gone by. We found it most enlightening!

**Naples Underground**
**Phone Number:** +39 081 296 944
http://www.napolisotterranea.org/en/naples-underground


And if you find yourself in Sorrento, we also think you'll love the **Viator's Eat Pray and Love Naples: Day Trip From Sorrento!** A knowledgeable, local guide takes you on this full day tour of Naples that's perfect for families and traveling groups of friends. Don't miss it!

**Eat Pray and Love Naples: Day Trip From Sorrento**
**Phone Number:** 1-888-651-9785
http://www.viator.com/tours/Sorrento/Eat-Pray-and-Love-Naples-Day-Trip-from-Sorrento/d947-7809P2

# • 5 Days in Naples & the Amalfi Coast! •

**Enjoy this 5-day itinerary** for a well-balanced and easy-going experience! There is plenty of room for **mixing and matching** our recommendations, so you can modify or adjust your itinerary in the interests of time, personal preference or convenience.

**Be sure to call ahead and check websites** for reservations, current pricing information and other details, as these are always subject to change. Enjoy!

## • Day 1 •

**Whether or not you chose to fly into Rome** and transfer to Naples, Sorrento or any of the other coastal towns on the Amalfi Coast, we recommend getting in **as early as possible** on your first day. It will be a long day of traveling and you may well have jet lag to overcome.

The earlier you arrive, the easier you may find it to fall in with local time.

**Once you arrive** at your hotel (or wherever you're staying) relax a bit, get settled, then freshen up before venturing out to explore the surrounding area.

**Most people begin in Naples**, and since it's the birthplace of pizza, we recommend lunch or dinner tonight at **L'Antica Pizzeria Da Michele.** Da Michele is known for making two classic pie styles: margherita and marinara — both flavorful and delicious! You'll most likely want to come back.

**And for dessert**, you can't be visiting Italy's Campania region without having *sfogliatella*, their signature pastry — light layers of flaky pastry dough on the outside, and  abundantly filled with sweetened ricotta cheese on the inside...you can thank us later! For this head over to **La Sfogliatella Mary** if happen to be in Naples, otherwise just ask someone where the best sfogliatella is in the town you're in!

**Another must dine option** any night you're in Naples is **Don Alfonso 1890!** Some say it's almost sacrilegious to visit southern Italy without dining in this delicious restaurant. Open since 1890, Don Alfonso's scrumptious dishes are prepared in the high style of French fare. The restaurant owners also have their own farmhouse from which they grow most of their own ingredients! This spot is not one to miss — so be sure to book a table well in advance!

## Location Information:

**L'Antica Pizzeria da Michele**
**Address:** Via Cesare Sersale, 1/3, 80139, Naples
**Phone Number:** +39 081 553 9204
http://www.damichele.net/index.php?lang=uk

**La Sfogliatella Mary**
**Address:** Via Toledo, 66, 80134, Naples
**Phone Number:** +39 081 402 218

**Don Alfonso 1890**
**Address:** Corso Sant'Agata, 11/13, 80064, Sant'Agata Sui Due Golfi, Naples
**Phone Number**: +39 081 878 0026
http://www.donalfonso.com/contatti.asp?lingua=ing

# • Day 2 •

**After a nice breakfast** at your hotel (or at **La Sfogliatella Mary** if you're in Naples!) Start the morning with a visit to **Museo Cappella Sansevero** (Sansevero Chapel Museum). Don't miss a view of the famous sculpture of The Veiled Christ and many other historical masterpieces.

**We recommend lunch** at the nearby **Tandem** restaurant. This area is one of the oldest in Naples, but they have very tasty ragu here, it's delish!

**Alternatively**, today would be perfect for a picnic. Just make an AM visit to Naples' **La Pignasecca** market. They open around 8:00 am and close early in the afternoon, between noon and 1:00 pm.

**And after lunch**, why not take the **Naples Underground** tour? Dip down over 130 feet back into the days of the ancient Greeks and Romans, with a guided below ground tour of the Historic Center of Naples — you may be surprised what there is to discover!

**And how about a night** at Italy's biggest and oldest opera house? A night at **Teatro di San Carlo** is always magical. The production season runs from January to December, with a break in the summer. Be sure to book your tickets well in advance.

**For dinner tonight** (before or after the theatre) we think you'll enjoy the family feel of the nearby **Osteria Il Gobbetto**. The menu is traditional Neapolitan fare, and they serve some of the best tasting food in Naples!

**Do get a good night's rest** because tomorrow you're off to the coast!

## Location Information:

**Sansevero Chapel Museum**
**Address:** Via F. De Sanctis 19/21, 80134, Naples
**Phone Number:** + 39 081 551 8470
http://www.museosansevero.it/en

**Tandem (Restaurant)**
**Address:** Via G. Paladino 51, 80138, Naples
**Phone Number:** +39 081 1900 2468

**Naples Underground**
**Phone Number:** +39 081 296 944
http://www.napolisotterranea.org/en/naples-underground

**La Pignasecca**
**Address:** Via Pignasecca, 80134, Naples

**Teatro di San Carlo**
**Address:** Via San Carlo 98, 80132, Naples, Italy
**Phone Number:** +39 081 797 2331 or +39 081 797 2111
http://www.teatrosancarlo.it/en

**Osteria Il Gobbetto (Restaurant)**
**Address:** Via Sergente Maggiore, 8, 80132, Naples
**Phone Number:** +39 081 251 2435

## • Day 3 •

**Today it's time to hit the gorgeous Amalfi Coast!** You can choose to spend a night or two there, or just take a day or group trip. We generally prefer to visit the Amalfi Coast rather than staying overnight, because although the towns are postcard pretty, they tend to be overcrowded with tourists—complete with tourist-geared pricing.

So, we think the best way to experience the coast initially is with Viator's full 8-hour day tour of the towns of **Sorrento, Positano, Amalfi, and Ravello!** You'll have a private chauffeur and English-speaking guide pick you up from your hotel in Naples and whisk you away for the day of a lifetime! You can see which area you like best and plan a return visit.

Should you happen to spend some additional time in **Positano**, you can't miss a visit to **Spiaggia Grande**, the "large beach" where everybody loves to hang out and relax, from the famous to the infamous!

**If you have dinner in Positano**, head over to **Da Vincenzo's!** A wonderful presentation and a delicious menu of Italian fare you'll devour in no time flat!

## Location Information:

Viator's Private Tour: Sorrento, Positano, Amalfi and Ravello Day Trip From Naples
Phone Number: 1-888-651-9785

http://www.viator.com/tours/Naples/Private-Tour-Sorrento-Positano-Amalfi-and-Ravello-Day-Trip-from-Naples/d508-2958AMAPV

**Spiaggia Grande (Beach)**
**Address:** Piazza Flavio Gioia, Positano, Italy

**Da Vincenzo**
**Address:** Via Pasitea, 172/178, 84017, Positano
**Phone Number:** +39 089 875 128
http://www.davincenzo.it

# • Day 4 •

**Ready for another day trip?** Great, because today you're visiting the spectacular island of Capri! It's the perfect day for Tours of Capri's **Capri Island Guided Tour!**

Some of Capri's main features are the amazingly gorgeous and azure-glowing **Blue Grotto** sea cave; the **Marina Piccola**, where according to Greek mythology, the sirens seduced Odysseus (Ulysses); the **Belvedere di Tragara** a panoramic seafront lined with the most beautiful villas—and many other highly trafficked sites!

As with the Amalfi Coast region in general, tourism is particularly high on the island of Capri, but the sightseeing is more than worth it—**just bring an extra dose of patience** with you and you'll have a wonderful experience!

**While in Capri**, try one of our favorite restaurants in town, **La Palette Bar Ristorante**. In addition to the amazing food, we really love the atmosphere here, not to mention some of the most gorgeous views on the island.

**An alternate itinerary** option is a day trip to the ancient ruins of **Pompeii**! We recommend booking Tours of Capri's **Ancient Pompeii Guided Tour** from Naples, and remember the tour fills up fast, so you'll need to book your tickets well in advance.

## Location Information:

Tours of Capri: Capri Island Guided Tour
Phone Number: +39 338 282 4366
http://www.toursofcapri.com/capriislandtour.html

**La Palette Bar Ristorante**
**Address:** Via Matermania, 36, 80073, Island of Capri, Italy
**Phone Number:** +39 081 837 9235
http://www.lapalette.it

**Tours of Capri: Ancient Pompeii Guided Tour**
**Phone Number:** +39 338 282 4366
http://www.toursofcapri.com/pompeiitour.html - ad-image-0

# • Day 5 •

**Unless you've stayed** over on the coast or schedule another day trip, plan to visit **Castel Nuovo** in Naples today, a large medieval fortress in front of city hall. Inside you'll find the **Civic Museum of Castel Nuovo** (Museo Civico), where an amazing variety of 14th- to 15th-century frescoes and sculptures (among other well preserved works) are displayed.

**For lunch today,** check out the nearby **Trattoria Castel Nuovo Pizzeria.** It's a humble atmosphere that serves up tasty and authentic Neapolitan treats you'll enjoy!

**And if you're up for a relaxing and refreshing afternoon**, visit the **Botanical Garden of Naples** (Orto Botanico di Napoli), a 19th century city staple containing the most soothing and enchanting flowers and fernery in Naples; entry is completely free of charge.

Why not schedule a **private boat tour** for the latter part of today? We highly recommend any one of **Capitano Ago's** wonderful excursions, depending on your likes and preferences. It's the perfect way to wrap up a wonderful week in Italy!

## Location Information:

**Civic Museum of Castel Nuovo**
**Address:** Piazza Castello, Naples
**Phone Number:** +39 081 795 7713

**Botanical Garden of Naples**
**Address:** Via Foria, 223, 80139, Naples

**Phone Number:** +39 081 253 3937
http://www.ortobotanico.unina.it/indexE.htm

**Trattoria Castel Nuovo Pizzeria**
**Address:** Piazza Francese 42, 80133, Naples
**Phone Number:** +39 081 551 5524
http://www.trattoriacastelnuovo.com

**Capitano Ago**
**Address:** Via Marina Grande, 92, 80067, Sorrento
**Phone Number:** +39 392 272 8910
http://www.capitanoago.com

# • Best Places For Travelers on a Budget •

**There are always plenty** of low cost options in Naples and in the various towns of the Amalfi Coast. Below we share our personal favorites for the best value, dollar-for-dollar.

**Be sure to call ahead and check websites** for availability and current prices, as these are always subject to change.

## Bargain Italian Sleeps

**One of the best values** in all of Naples is definitely **Week-end a Napoli.** This boutique hotel villa is in Vomero Hill, an exclusive neighborhood in Naples, and it's not far from the subway and railway terminals. With only 8 rooms, you'll need to book well in advance to secure a spot here for your time in Naples.

**Week-end a Napoli**
**Address:** Via Enrico Alvino 157, 80129, Naples
**Phone Number:** +39 081 578 1010
http://www.weekendanapoli.com

**Our second top recommendation** for a budget option in Naples is **Hotel Il Convento.** Although conveniently located in the heart of the city, this hotel is still quite affordable. Rooms are elegant and cozy, with discount packages offered on a regular basis.

**Hotel Il Convento**
**Address:** Via Speranzella 137/A 80132, Naples
**Phone Number:** +39 081 403 977
http://www.hotelilconvento.it/HomeEn.html


**For a nice, clean affordable option in Sorrento**, we recommend the **Ulisse Deluxe Hostel**. Centrally located for great sightseeing, this hostel has all the great amenities of a fine three-star hotel at a great value. You'll be very comfortable here.

**Ulisse Deluxe Hostel**
**Address:** Via del Mare, 22, 80067, Sorrento
**Phone Number:** +39 081 877 4753
http://www.ulissedeluxe.com


**In Positano**, we recommend **Pensione Maria Luisa**. Book a budget stay here for some of the most priceless views on the Amalfi Coast! There are a few other reasons to stay here as well, such as the clean, spacious rooms, and the warm, friendly hospitality.

**Pensione Maria Luisa**
**Address:** Via Fornillo 42, 84017, Positano
**Phone Number:** +39 089 875 023
http://www.pensionemarialuisa.com


**For those looking to stay a night or two (or more) in Capri** without blowing their budget, our top recommendation is **La Tosca, Capri**. In this intimate, family-run hotel you enjoy the gorgeous, picturesque landscape without the hefty price tag.

**La Tosca, Capri**
**Address:** Via Dalmazio Birago, 5, 80073, Capri
**Phone Number:** +39 081 837 0989
http://www.latoscahotel.com

**And if you're looking** for the perfect budget hotel in the town of **Amalfi** itself, we suggest **La Pergola**, another small family-run hotel with breathtaking views, clean rooms, delicious food and warm, friendly hosts.

 **La Pergola**
**Address:** via Giovanni Augustariccio 10, 84011, Amalfi
**Phone Number:** +39 089 831 088
http://www.lapergolamalfi.it/en

## Bargain Italian Eats

**L'Antica Pizzeria Da Michele** in Naples is known for their super affordable classic pie styles: margherita and marinara — we love both and know you will too!

**L'Antica Pizzeria da Michele**
**Address:** Via Cesare Sersale, 1/3, 80139, Naples
**Phone Number:** +39 081 553 9204
http://www.damichele.net/index.php?lang=uk

**Trattoria a' Pignata** is also a delicious Neapolitan choice for a great value. Serving great seafood and Neapolitan fare and run by a sweet couple, the hospitality here can't be beat...unless it's by the affordable prices!

**Trattoria a' Pignata**
**Address:** Vico Lungo del Gelso, 110/112, 80134, Naples
**Phone Number:** +39 081 038 3437
http://www.trattoriapignata.it

**In Sorrento**, don't miss the **Foreigner's Club!** Delicious Italian food at more than reasonable prices. There's even a resident wedding planner for weddings on the terrace overlooking the Gulf of Naples, so the place gets pretty busy, but the food is definitely worth it!

**Foreigner's Club - Sorrento**
**Address:** Via Luigi De Maio 35, 80067, Sorrento
**Phone Number:** +39 081 877 3263
http://www.circolodeiforestieri.com/en

**If you're spending time in Capri** and looking for a tasty budget option, **Buca di Bacco** is our favorite! They're small and busy but they serve really delicious, authentic Italian pizza favorites.

**Buca di Bacco**
**Address:** Via Longano, 35, 80073, Capri, Island of Capri
**Phone Number:** +39 081 837 0723
http://www.capri.com/en/c/buca-di-bacco-3

# • Best Places For Ultimate Luxury •

There are many luxurious hotels and restaurants in Naples and throughout the extensive Amalfi Coast, and we're excited to share our favorite high-end accommodations and fine dining spots along the coast!

**Remember to call ahead** or check websites for current rates and availability. Most of these accommodations fill up quickly year-round, so you may need to make reservations months in advance to secure rooms and suites!

## Luxury Italian Sleeps

**If you're looking for luxury in Naples**, don't miss the **Palazzo Decumani**, a 19th-century palace turned charming, luxurious hotel in the heart of the city. The location is fabulous—you're close to just about everything worth seeing in Naples!

**Palazzo Decumani**
**Address:** Via del Grande Archivio, 8, 80100, Naples
**Phone Number:** +39 081 420 1379
http://www.palazzodecumani.com/en/index

**And while there are also many good luxury options in Positano**, we're in love with **Le Sirenuse**. You can't go wrong here! Naturally the views are mesmerizing, everything is top notch and the staff is eager to pamper and attend to your every need. Pure heaven awaits you at Le Sirenuse.

**Le Sirenuse**
**Address:** Via C. Colombo, 30, 84017, Positano
**Phone Number:** +39 089 87 50 66
http://www.sirenuse.it/en/13/default.aspx

**In Amalfi, Hotel Marina Riviera** is the place to be. Although a 4-star hotel, we think it is more charming and better located than its 5-star rivals. A popular accommodation for honeymooners, a stay at Hotel Marina is akin to being in paradise!

**Hotel Marina Riviera**
**Address:** Via Pantaleone Comite 19, 84011, Amalfi
**Phone Number:** +39 089 871 104
http://www.marinariviera.it

**In Capri**, there's no better place to stay in our opinion than **Hotel Caesar Augustus**. Their slogan says it all: "Never settle for less than your dreams."

**Caesar Augustus**
**Address:** Via G. Orlandi, 4 | Baia de Napoli, 80071, Anacapri, Island of Capri
**Phone Number:** +39 081 837 3395
http://www.caesar-augustus.com

## Luxury Italian Eats

**Sushi lovers** will be in heaven at **'O Sushi** in Naples. The creativity here is amazing and makes for a culinary experience you must be sure to overindulge in!

**'O Sushi**
**Address:** Via Francesco Cilea 203/207, 80127, Naples
**Phone Number:** +39 081 049 4464
http://www.osushi.it

**And while in Naples**, don't miss a truly delectable dining treat at **Don Alfonso 1890.** You can't visit southern Italy without having a meal at Don Alfonso's legendary restaurant!

**Don Alfonso 1890**
**Address:** Corso Sant'Agata, 11/13, 80064, Sant'Agata Sui Due Golfi, Naples
**Phone Number**: +39 081 878 0026
http://www.donalfonso.com/contatti.asp?lingua=ing

**In Sorrento,** our favorite high-end Italian cuisine is at **Ristorante Bagni Delfino.** They tend to be a seasonal operation, so you must call ahead for reservations. Catch them when they're open, it's amazing to eat here!

**Ristorante Bagni Delfino**
**Address:** Via Marina Grande, 216, 80067, Sorrento
**Phone Number:** +39 081 878 2038

**In Positano,** we think the luxury dining is best at **Da Vincenzo!** Wonderful presentation and a delicious menu of Italian fare you'll devour in no time flat.

**Da Vincenzo**
**Address:** Via Pasitea, 172/178, 84017, Positano
**Phone Number:** +39 089 875 128
http://www.davincenzo.it

**In Capri**, you'll love **Da Tonino**. Fine dining at its best. It's a bit of a walk to get here, but the effort will be well worth it.

**Da Tonino**
**Address:** Via Dentecala, 15, Capri, Island of Capri
**Phone Number:** +39 081 837 6718
http://www.ristorantedatonino.it

# • Naples & the Amalfi Coast Nightlife •

**Please note** that in Italy, the words "bar" and "café" are interchangeable, so be sure to specify what you're looking for when asking for recommendations from locals. Most hotel staff will know the difference.

## Great Bars in Naples & the Amalfi Coast

**Enoteca Belledonne** is a great little wine bar in Naples' upscale Chiaia area. It's a very nice atmosphere with a great wine list and even better snacking.

**Enoteca Belledonne**
**Address:** Vico Belledonne a Chiaia 18, Naples
**Phone Number:** +39 081 403 162
http://www.enotecabelledonne.com/default.aspx

**The best in upscale nightlife on the Amalfi Coast** in our opinion is in Positano! Our top recommendation is the **Champagne & Oyster Bar** at Le Sirenuse hotel. Have a nice drink while taking in the stunning views and rubbing shoulders with the who's who!

**Champagne & Oyster Bar**
**Address:** Le Sirenuse Hotel | Via Cristoforo Colombo, 30, 84017, Positano
**Phone Number:** 39 089 875 066
http://sirenuse.it/en/86/champagne---oyster-bar.aspx

**When in Capri**, everyone knows the best spot for drinks after dark is **Buca di Bacco.** You may even run into a few celebrities while you're there!

**Buca di Bacco**
**Address:** Via Longano, 35, 80073, Capri, Island of Capri
**Phone Number:** +39 081 837 0723
http://www.capri.com/en/c/buca-di-bacco-3

# Great Clubs in Naples & the Amalfi Coast

**One of the best dance clubs** in Naples is **Teatro Posillipo**—a trendy spot with unlimited disco music, a great vibe and the promise of a fun-filled night on the town.

**Teatro Posillipo**
**Address:** Via Posillipo, 66, 80123, Naples
**Phone Number:** +39 081 1954 4344
http://www.teatroposillipo.it

Outside of Naples, nightlife tends to focus in on Positano, specifically at **Music on the Rocks!** It's a multi-leveled hot spot where even locals go for a great night out. Check their website for upcoming events, as there's always a full calendar!

**Music on the Rocks**
**Address:** Via Grotte dell'incanto 51, Positano
**Phone Number:** + 39 089 875 874
http://www.musicontherocks.it/home.php

# Great Live Music in Naples & the Amalfi Coast

**New Around Midnight** is the hottest jazz club in Naples. Friday and Saturday are the best nights to visit for great live performances, and you must book in advance to ensure you'll have a table.

**New Around Midnight**
**Address:** Via Giuseppe Bonito, 32, 80100, Naples
**Phone Number:** +39 081 558 2834
http://www.newaroundmidnight.it

**You should also hang out at Goodfellas**, for a creative atmosphere and décor, and a nice range of live entertainment to suit all music tastes.

**Goodfellas**
**Address:** Via Morghen 34, 80100, Naples
**Phone Number:** +39 340 922 5475
http://www.goodfellasclub.com

The world famous **Africana** nightclub is also not to be missed if you're on the Amalfi Coast. This hot spot has played host to the likes of Aristotle Onassis and Jackie Kennedy and it's still one of the best places to be for a great night on the town!

**Africana Famous Club**
**Address:** Via Terramare 2, 84010, Praiano
**Phone Number:** +39 089 874 858
http://www.africanafamousclub.com

## Great Theatre in Naples & the Amalfi Coast

**The best place for good theatre performances** in southern Italy is definitely Naples' **Teatro di San Carlo.** The production season runs from January to December, with a break in the summer. Be sure to book your tickets well in advance!

**Teatro di San Carlo**
**Address:** Via San Carlo 98, 80132, Naples
**Phone Number:** +39 081 797 2331 or +39 081 797 2111
http://www.teatrosancarlo.it/en

# • Conclusion •

**Naples is quickly** becoming one of Italy's first-choice destinations, on par with Rome, Florence, Venice or Milan. And southern Italy's **Amalfi** coastline will always be home to some of the most beautiful towns in Italy, all with much to offer their visitors.

**So we hope you have found** our guide to Italy's magnificent Campania region and its southern coastal cities helpful, and wish you a safe, memorable, and fun-filled trip to Naples and the Amalfi Coast!

Ciao!

**The Passport to European Travel Guides Team**

**Visit our Blog!** Grab more of our signature guides for all your travel needs!

http://www.passporttoeuropeantravelguides.blogspot.com

★ **Join our mailing list** ★ to follow our Travel Guide Series. You'll be automatically entered for a chance to win a **$100 Visa Gift Card** in our monthly drawings! Be sure to respond to the confirmation e-mail to complete the subscription.

• **About the Authors** •

**Passport to European Travel Guides** is an eclectic team of international jet setters who know exactly what travelers and tourists want in a cut-to-the-chase, comprehensive travel guide that suits a wide range of budgets.

Our growing collection of distinguished European travel guides is guaranteed to give first-hand insight to each locale, complete with day-to-day, guided itineraries you won't want to miss!

We want our brand to be your official Passport to European Travel — one you can always count on!

Bon Voyage!

The Passport to European Travel Guides Team
http://www.passporttoeuropeantravelguides.blogspot.com

Lightning Source UK Ltd.
Milton Keynes UK
UKHW02f1929130718
325690UK00021B/706/P